HEAVENS PROMISE

by Paolo Hewitt

This book is dedicated to the following without whom. . . . .

Sarah Jane, (One day we will be free),
Stephanie Hardy, for a love supreme,
My own Brother P. for enduring loyalty and wisdom
The Supino famiglia from here to Sorrento,
Jeff Barrett for spotting the potential,
And to an extraordinary circle of friends who, without a
word being said, gathered around and caught me
everytime I fell. Love and happiness to each and every one.

HEAVENS PROMISE

by Paolo Hewitt

Published by **HEAVENLY**

Jacket Designed by
Pete Barrett.

Painting by
Johnny Chandler.

Photo by
Chris Clunn.

Typography and
design by
Carol Briggs

Edited by
Kevin Pearce

Published by
HEAVENLY
72 Wardour Street
London
WC2

Printed by
Woolnough
Bookbinding Ltd

ISBN 0-9520721-1-4

PART ONE

COLOUR ME LONDON

Early 1988

Looking back on it now and having been granted a somewhat sensitive impulse, a bitter sweet quality that can bring both joy and pain into one's daily runnings, it was not strange to me that when the phone started up in my yard that Saturday morning, I somehow knew my world was going to change forever.

This was not, I hasten to add, a fully formed clear-as-blue thought that came into my mind's eye but one which flashed by with very liitle attention paid to its distant, rainbow like journey. It was only much later that my HQ, in its inimitable and unique style, ran past me again this distant premonition thus prompting the putting of pen to paper.

I should also state that when the phone kicked sharply into life I was hardly in full control of my wide and diverse facilities, given the relatively early nature of the day. It takes space, solitude and numerous coffee cups to clear the fog of sleep from my mind and prepare me for the events ahead, and it is not until the clock has slipped an hour that I become fully compos mentis and ready for whatever the world wants to throw at me and, of course, vice versa.

It was 10.30 in the a.m. when I picked up the receiver and killed the phone's shrill noise, situated as I was in the front room of my small London abode.

"Yep."

"It's Sandra."

This was a gal that I had been seeing off and on, on and off, over the past few weeks and if truth be told my feelings towards her were hardly of the Romeo and Juliet type such as you can occasionally see in certain couples who, lost in the glow of new found love, can hardly walk ten yards down the road without loving each other up.

"Oh hi," I replied, "how's it going?"

"Fine. I'm pregnant."

"You are what?"

"I said, I am pregnant."

I have sometimes wondered in my numerous day dreams, when my HQ gladly pushes reality aside to conjure up all manner of fanciful thoughts, how I would feel if I was ever confronted with the words that Sandra had just used and, although I took the painful and, let's face it, not exactly the cleverest route to answering that quesion, I can at least jot down the answer now with complete and utter certainty.

Numb. Your body and mind turn numb. Every emotion or feeling inside instantly ices over and your mind, like a TV as it's just been switched off, goes blank, unless, of course, the gal in question is your fulltime squeeze and you planned the whole caboodle from start to finish. This, I have to relate, was not my position and so I said the first thing that came to mind.

"Is it mine?"

"You fucking bastard, I knew you'd say that. Who do you think I am?" she demanded.

I realised my error and quickly scrambled for cover although there was some logic behind my question. In the nature of a casual affair, which is how I read it, I have always been of the notion that neither partner can really make claims on the other's runnings.

Where Sandra went and how she conducted her time when she was away from me was down to her and her alone.

"I'm sorry," I said, "I didn't it mean that way."

An uncomfortable silence settled in between us, each waiting for the other to speak. Sandra finally went first.

"Well, hot shot, got anything to say or has the cat got your tongue?"

"I thought you were taking precautions. We talked about it."

"They failed."

I couldn't help but think, right then and there as I held the phone in disbelief, just how seriously unpredictable life can be. A piece of rubber snaps in half and suddenly two people are hurtling down a road they never knew existed, their lives turned upside down and careering towards who knew where.

"Aren't you happy?" Sandra asked in a tentative tone, her voice tailing off. I really couldn't tell if she was joking or not but knowing the quick silver temper that I have seen rear up in her on a couple of occasions I thought it best not to ask.

If the truth be known, I was actually praying that this was a huge wind up being played out at my expense and in a few seconds Sandra would burst into laughter and this whole nightmare would be over. Which is the kind of desperate thinking you get into when something appears out of the nowhere blue and knocks you clean off your feet with a force that is ten times your strength.

"Well, we'd better meet," I heard her say, the words cutting through the air of silence and shock that I was being forced to breathe in.

"No, now now, not today," I quickly replied. "I'm busy all over the weekend."

This was not a true statement on my behalf but I needed time to stall and get myself and my thoughts together.

"How you fixed up Monday?"

There was no answer and I suddenly imagined her sitting at her yard, a sinking feeling opening up her stomach as she came to realise that I was not the best person to have been recruited for the job of fatherhood.

"Call me first thing, Monday. Alright?"

I held the phone carefully and then she exploded

"No, it's not alright you bastard. You fucking well call me."

Sandra smashed down the phone and the line crashed. I put down the phone and sat there in complete silence, unable to believe what had just passed. I reached for a cigarette, sparked up and then swung back into action. Picking up the phone, I hit a number and twenty seconds later, much to my relief, my closest confidant, the Brother P. came on the line.

I can't tell you how glad I was to find him for he is an elusive man and very prone towards the unpredictable, this being one of the reasons I dig him.

"P. man, it's me. We need a meet fast."

"Yeah?" came his cool reply delivered as if it was a question, "Papa's in an hour?"

"That's the one. Check you then."

Putting the phone to rest, I snapped on the answer machine. I desperately wanted to clear the buzzing in my head and had no inclination whatsoever to parlare with anyone else, especially if Sandra took it upon herself to call back.

I have to say here that what did me up the most was Sandra's little line about being happy as if on receiving her disaster bulletin she somehow expected that I would be hiring out the Royal Albert Hall to celebrate.

How she got to that point I have no idea but what I do know, to paint a clearer picture, is that this loose link between us had started at The Unity Club where I can be found DJ'ing three nights a week, this being my chosen profession and how I am able to provide a roof over my head, foodage on the table, gears in the wardrobe and enough tunes to keep me happy and employable. I had only just started spinning there having gained the job through a lucky squeeze. Costello, the club's middle aged and gruff manager, had caught the club's regular DJ with his headphones around his neck and his hands in the till and personally marched him out of the club. Appealing to the Brother P., the boy to call when such situations arise, and who, as fate would have it, luckily happened to be present and correct that night, for assistance, my main link dialled my number and I have held down the post ever since. On my fourth nervous night there, as it is not often that such golden chances arise, Jill, who works the cloakroom, brought a drink and a friend up to the booth.

"This is Sandra," she announced, clutching her arm.

"She's a good friend of mine and she wants to know if you will play a record for her, and because you're such a good DJ and a sweetie to boot, I told her that I'm sure you would."

I made a slight grimace for Jill, a small, blond haired gal with a wide smile and unflappable nature, which comes in very useful when fifty people are rushing to get their coats and then home, knows as well as I do that this asking for records business is something every DJ hates.

It's either odds on that he or she hasn't got the tune in question or, if they have, it is always one that will automatically kill stone dead the mood they are trying to build.

"Oh, forget it," Sandra said, noting my small expression of disapproval and starting to turn away. "You probably haven't got it anyway."

Now there are many things you can say to a DJ but if you really want to get to him or her, just simply suggest that their collection is not up to par and then retire ten yards after lighting. Shame to say it but DJ's are by nature's cruel design zealous hoarders of vinyl, self obsessed individuals who always want to be one step ahead of the pack and who see nothing wrong in dedicating their lives and cashola to building up an unrivalled amount of tunes, this being their version of the Holy Grail and how to achieve meaning in life.

They are also not above telling out and out lies about tunes they claim to possess and even I have to plead guilty on that score.

"That Billy Brooks track? Yeah, I know it. Got it a few months back. Safe track, man."

To be shamed in front of your peers for not owning a current hot tune that everyone is parlaring about always brought back that unwelcome feeling you got back in school, when your P&M couldn't or wouldn't buy you the latest gears and you walked around for days cut off from everybody.

You have to keep face and that is why heaven to a DJ is finding a record that no one else is onto and letting it loose upon the crowd you play to because, believe it, if it's a great enough tune, in no time at all it will be the record on everyone's lips and, what's more, your name is associated with it. That's what gives you the juice in this game and what you are always aiming for.

So to publicly doubt me, as Sandra had just done, was guaranteed to spark me off but before I could properly respond to her challenge, I have to say that I was thrown off course by the little smile that was playing on her mouth and starting to intrigue me, myself and I.

"What tune is it?" I asked, acting bored while all the time slyly taking in the rest of her appearance which, I must state, was not an unpleasant experience given her large, dark brown eyes, the casual simplicity of her dress, smart white t shirt and faded Levis, and the languid movement of her legs as her and Jill made to walk away.

"It's called 'Nobody But You Babe,' by Clarence Reid," she said over her shoulder.

It was a class request, no doubt on that one, but it was stacked away at my yard and out of sight.

"I've got it at home, if that's any good to you," I replied.

"How nice for you, dear." Sandra motioned to the dex behind me with raised eyebrows.

"By the way," she said, "the tune you're playing is about to finish."

Turning to the dex in a panic, I hastily mixed in another tune, and not too badly either if I don't say so myself, for the dancers out on the floor, and there were some serious movers in the house that night, failed to notice the join and kept to the groove, thankfully not deserting the dancefloor in huge numbers, the nightmare that haunts every DJ who is playing out and one which the Brother P. once termed as the playing of the Moses Record.

That's when you play a tune that is so wack and wrong that the crowd out on the floor suddenly part like the Red Sea and leave you playing to a deserted floor.

When I looked back Sandra had floated away and I had two chances of spotting her, little and none. The Unity Club, let me explain, is a tight, dank venue where naked pipes run across all the walls and constantly drip-drip-drip, oozing condensation.

Behind my booth, there is a bar area with tables and chairs to rest upon. In front of me is the small sized dance arena where the people pack in tight, rubbing, touching, sweating and expressing themselves to the music. The faint smell of sex is everywhere and anywhere, and from my raised booth I can hardly make out the faces as they move through the gloomy light like ghosts, so I knew I'd lost Sandra swallowed up as she was by the darkness and the crowd.

She would either have to come over to me or I would have to wait for the last tune and lights up to locate her, so I put her out of my mind's frame and concentrated on my DJ'ing. This is a skill which I look upon as a true art form, although I know many people don't even think about the DJ, in the way you get on a bus and never check the driver until they do something mad like take a bend at 80, which is when you sit up and take notice.

But for me, myself and I, DJ'ing is one of the few things in life that really moves me. To be able to play your record collection to a crowd of people and see them respond favourably, is not only to have your taste vindicated but can actually, when the crowd is moving as one, be quite a moving sight.

My faves, and I don't mean to be unpatriotic and all that, are the Americans for I have heard bootleg tapes from New York and it's unbelievable what some of them cats get up to. I work off two dex, which is hard enough, but these dudes double that amount and you still can not hear them mixing from one record to another because somehow, they keep the beat steady and constant, and one day, when the cashola is there, I have determined to fly over and discover their secrets.

Switching my attention back to the job at hand, I decided to go into my favourite mix, a musical concotion that I had put together at home on my two SL 1200 turntables and which featured "Raw" by Big Daddy Kane, "I Know You Got Soul" by Bobby Byrd, "Rebel Without A Pause" by Public Enemy, James Brown's "Stone To The Bone," Sly Stone's "If You Want Me To Stay," Cymande's "The Message" before heading back to the present with Eric B. and Rakim's "Microphone Fiend."

As I was searching out the next tune whilst also thinking what a powerful force music is and how it can really help you deal with the stress and strain of Capital living by allowing you to let off big time on the dancefloor, I noticed a compilation LP I had just picked up on the cheap and which featured the tune Sandra had asked for, all present and correct on side one, track 4.

I pulled it out, mixed it in and within thirty seconds of the tune finishing, there was sweet Sandra standing beside me, saying, "I thought you said it was at home."

"It was," I replied, "but I ran home to get it for you."

"Fetch me a bucket," she said with a laugh that lit up her face.

"Eddie Bo," I replied.

"What?"

"Eddie Bo. He cut a tune called 'Check The Bucket.' I forget which label."

"How absolutely fascinating. And I suppose that record is at home as well."

"Third shelf, on the left hand side. Where do you live?"

Sandra hesitated for a moment. "North."

"Well, if you want to share a cab after, you can pop in and meet the great Eddie Bo."

"I think I can live without that dubious privilege," she replied.

"But we can share a cab if you like."

This we did but if you're wondering what came next, let me tell you straight away, people, that nothing happened that first night except for some pleasant chit chat in the back of the cab.

It was the following night when it all went off. Sandra unexpectedly called round, ("the friend I went to see was out...") and, after a couple of brews and a few smokes, I picked up the courage to pull the following stunt, taught to me, myself and I by the first number at our school, an Italian number called Enzo, to lose his cherry, much to our great consternation and extreme astonishment.

Now, believe me, I know the following yarn sounds a bit silly in the cold light of day but it does work so I'll put it down and you can make of it what you will.

"What you do," Enzo explained to a group of us hanging onto his every word as if he was the Messiah just descended, which to many of us he was as he'd just pulled off something that the rest of us could only think about, "is you sit on the sofa with her and about halfway through the evening pick up her hand and say, that's a nice ring you're wearing. Keep holding her hand. After she's said, yes, so and so gave it to me, either she'll pull her hand away, in which case forget it, or she will let you hold on, which means you're in."

Sandra let me hold her hand but the nerves between the both of us could have kept this town's electricity supply alive for a 100 years until, unable to stand the tension anymore, I made a move and we began kissing.

Sad to say but my first romp with Sandra was not the starry eyed experience that you always hope for when you couple up for the first time, but then how could it be when you consider that sex, nine times out of ten, only fires up after a real familiarity has been established, and you get to know each other and what is required, which is why I have to laugh everytime I go cinema and there, on the silver screen, the two leads fly at each other to a sound track of deafining moaning and groaning.

It's not the depiction that upsets me and far from it, because I'd much rather watch people loving it up than kicking ten shades out of each other any day of the year, but it's the obvious dishonesty of it all that bugs me, so much so, in fact, that if the keeper's of the nation's morals, Mrs. Mary W. and her army of knitting needles, were to campaign on this ticket, namely persuading the film numbers to depict how things really go down between people about to dip their feet in some of the deepest and strangest waters there are, why she'd have my vote each and every time.

As it was Sandra and I were fumbling and awkward with each other, failing badly to reach the fireworks stage and it struck me after, as I tried to drift off into dreamland and put behind me what had just passed, that the idea of sex with someone was sometimes far more of a kick than the act itself, and when you also considered the grief you saved both yourself and your partner, then maybe that would be the best course for me to charter over the next few months.

The problemo, of course, stemmed from that vital piece of man known as John Thomas. That incorrigible organ tends to direct a man's outlook a lot of the time and if every boy and girl was wised up to his ways and manners at a very early age, then you'd have the smartest, not to mention the happiest nation on earth. True thing, people.

Contemplating these thoughts I slipped into darkness and when I came to the next morning Sandra had flown the yard to get to work, leaving behind a name and number which I used the next night to invite her down to The Unity.

Indeed, the romping started to gear up between us but if truth be told it never hit full swing and that was down to me and the fact that I was still carrying a torch for the First Lady of my life, a state of being that I have only just come to terms with, although

Sandra sussed it almost straight away.

On our third night together, she said, "There's someone else isn't there?"

"No, there isn't," I said, taken aback a little.

"There is, I can tell."

"I promise you Sandra, I'm not checking anyone else."

"Just because you can't see it doesn't mean it's not there," she said cryptically, and not, I have to add, a little sadly.

"I don't know what you're talking about," I quickly said and then reached for her. She just sighed and now as I muse on it all I am left wondering if that was the night we created human life.

I shook the notion out of my head and glanced at the clock. 10.53 a.m. Time to get busy.

I moved into my small bedroom and perused my gears which hang on a rail that takes up one side of the room. I should explain here that gears, the art of acquiring an item and then presenting yourself to the world in an eye balling fashion, is a lifelong habit of mine and although the choosing of how best to dress for the day is one of my morning's better moments, that consideration for today, at least, was out of the window. Within two minutes I was dressed, gathering up my essentials for the day, which means cigarettes, keys, walkman, tapes, all of which are placed in a small bowling bag, and heading out of the door.

My yard is in North London, above a newsagents in fact, on the Stroud Green Road, a stretch of tar and pavement with a rambling selection of shops and dwellings on either side. As you might expect for someone of my limited means, my yard is small as there are but three small rooms to which I can keep myself and my belongings, the biggest space being taken up by the countless tunes I have gathered up over the years.

You will no doubt have sussed by now that for me, myself and I, music is one of the few reasons why I find existence on this earth so enjoyable, the simple reason being that not only is music capable of placing a lot of folk in a very cool mood, and that applies to each and everyone whether it be the sound of a church bell in the early morning mist or Miss Nina Simone testifying, but it can actually transcend normal life and take you out of yourself to a place that is unbelievably wondrous and inspiring.

Music can give you such a boost that from where I'm standing no drug has yet been invented to match it and that's why every day I go in search of a fix.It is also the reason why the walls of my yard are filled with pictorial tributes to those God given talents, Marvin Gaye, Al Green, Stevie Wonder, Donald Byrd, Donny Hathaway, The Isley Brothers, and many more, whose work will always ring down the decades, touching every guy and gal for as long as the world keeps turning.

In fact, after Sandra's call I had toyed with the idea of placing Miss Nina Simone's heartaching "Little Boy Blue" on the turntable to push me down so I could rise up higher, but instead, anxious not to be late, I rushed out of the yard and onto the concrete just as the Stroud Green Road was coming to life.

Saturday morning shoppers filled the pavement and buses, packed to the gills slowly manoevered between the parked cars, carrying some of the the locals to the tube and a day in the West End. An array of colourful plastic shopping bags flashed in front of my eyes like a surreal painting as the street started to stretch itself for the long day ahead, announcing its waking amidst much noise and bustle.

I have to say that this is a really cool area to be plotted up in. Uno, most of the street is really wide, such as you see in pics of cities like Rome or New York, and I likes the breathing space that gives you. Due, there's all kinds of shop business

happening here to suit all tastes and fancies. Record shops, books, bakeries, car showrooms, supermarkets, newsagents, florists, electrical goods, and even an old Gentleman's outfitters where, when you buy something, they write you out a receipt, ring up the price on an old wooden cash till and generally behave towards you as if you were Top Boy in a Noel Coward play.

Walk ten yards either side of this quaint bastion of a Britain Forgotten and you will come across a Chinese supermarket to the South and a Mauritian fish shop to the North, whilst if hunger should strike on your journey, you can, if funds are of a sufficient nature, mangare on Italian, Polish, Chinese or West Indian grub of the highest quality.

Throw in the different snippets of language that fly like birds up and down the road, mix in the the assortment of tantalising smells that emanate from all corners and which must whisk up so many memories for the people living and working around the way, and consider the undisputed truth that within this area there is rarely trouble or tension in the air, just a shared sense of living on the balance, and you'll understand my goodwill to the area and the fervent wish I harbour that such streets should be duplicated all over this green and pleasant land.

It was getting warmer as I headed towards the tube and as I slipped off my white Levi's jacket, Digger suddenly loomed into view from out of a doorway that is set back from the betting shop, this being the local drunk who spends his days walking up and down, up and down, the Stroud with a constant runny nose and a can of Special Brew that his long skinny fingers clutch tightly.

His cheeks are hollowed out and his hair has turned white. You can see he is still relatively young but streetlife survival has aged him twenty years at least. Shabby clothes cover his skinny body and he slurs his words into an indecipherable accent, a linguistic style which proved totally troublesome to moi on my very first encounter with him when he blasted, "SLIVEUS SLOME MONEY," directly into my face one rainy morning.

It took me 60 seconds in the pouring rain to translate his demand as, "give us some money," a fair enough request given the burden he has to bear, and I handed him some coinage over, as I have been doing ever since I took up residence in this part of the world.

Since we are on this tip, I must explain that several acquaintances of mine often reprimand me for such actions, telling me, "that kind will only drink it," as if someone like Digger can beg up enough cashola which will one day enable him to walk into an estate agent's, spread it all out on a table and grab a nice little semi out in the suburbs with the rest of the mortgage brigade.

An extreme I know but such attitudes often make me wonder about my fellow countryfolk for when it comes to feeding people who live thousands of miles away in a Godforsaken desert, living a life that you and I can't even begin to imagine, the British prove themselves each and every time.

No doubt about it, as soon as the call comes through and the TV screen is full of starving children and desperate mothers, they're up and away, raiding their hard earnt bank balances to give over to people they probably didn't even know existed the day before. You have to tip your hat to them because that kind of spirit speaks volumes and should always be celebrated.

Yet ask them to do the same for someone living on the street but 200 yards away from their doorstep and you suddenly start walking into remarks like, "well, it's their own fault," as if the folk in question had chosen that life as a kind of perverse career move and had now triumphantly achieved their ambitions in life.

When the stench of another's nightmare gets too close, we smell ourselves and run away in horror, but that is no solution and so before Digger had to ask, I reached into my pocket and handed over the loose change. Thank God, I thought for the perverse warm weather for it might just make today a little easier for Digger and his compadres and, passing that thought, I soon found myself at the tube station.

Walking down the long snaking tunnel to the grey dirty platforms, I passed numerous people out and about on their business and somehow the scene livelied me up somewhat, especially as the busker on the morning shift was a young, dude coming on strong with a nice selection of Bob Marley tunes. I went to give him a coin as I do anyone who is not playing the obvious songs for my rule on buskers is a fair one. Nothing at all against The Beatles or Bob Dylan or Simon and Garfunkel, because they've all done their bit, but if I hear one more crooner singing "Yesterday" or "Knocking On Heaven's Door" then I will have no option but to immediately report them to the nearest authorities for gross public misconduct, and that especially applies to "Theme From The Deer Hunter."

This morning's musical selection featured Marley's "One Love/ People Get Ready," and was sung with such conviction that you couldn't help but be moved by both singer and song.

Yet despite my good mood I soon found it to be temporary. Boarding the train to take me Westward Ho, the Sandra business reared up in my HQ and immediately took me right down. What hit me first, as I struggled to make sense of this morning's unexpected and unbelievable events, was that, without a doubt, all future missions, such as a stay in New York to crib off those DJ masters, were going to have to be put on ice until this crisis was sorted, one way or another.

That was for sure but there was something else starting to bug me out and that was a growing feeling that suddenly, I had no control whatsoever over my life. It was as if, like a terrible dream you have to wake yourself up from, I had become a lead character in a film I had no desire to be in and the director hadn't even told me the plot and dialogue and I was left to improvise like John Coltrane to make sense of it all.

Perhaps, I mused, that was precisely what life was, a huge mega budget epic with God directing us all purely for His own amusement, the biggest joke being that all us poor souls have been led to believe that we are somehow in charge of how the film starts and finishes.

No doubt about it, as the great Sam Cooke knew, a change was going to come and I would have to bend with it or lose badly and that was the truth, Ruth.

Only I didn't want to make that move and not when my runnings had finally started to come together. I had living quarters, cashola, a job which I could use as a springboard to the next level if I was sharp enough, but above all I had a certain kind of freedom which allowed me space in my life, a space that far too many are forced to give up the day they walk out of school and start taking orders from the bosses.

From an early age I had determined that I wanted no part of that nine to five scam and so, on the day I dumped my blazer where it belonged, I had put my all into becoming a DJ, dedicating all my spare hours to acquiring equipment and learning how best to use it, sharpening my skills so that I was not answerable to some greyer of a boss who would take delight in making your life a misery because his was so utterly sad.

To achieve that end I devised a routine that involves constantly tuning into the pirate radio stations scattered all over town, cluing up on various magazines for tip offs, visiting record shops at least three times a week, (except on Sundays when I head for record fairs or car boot sales) and forever using my HQ to put together various mixes in my head which I then try out at my yard where no one is looking.

Consequently, I am on first name terms with a lot of shop owners and fellow DJ's and many hours are spent talking over music, artists, name producers, record labels, new releases, old tunes discovered, clubs, musicians and anything else connected to this vast and rich world that I so delight in being a part of.

If others can't check for these lengthy conversations then they are deemed irrelevants although it must be stated that, on the whole, women are the exception to the rule. Gals like music a lot but the majority of them use it differently, and without the obssesion.

It is of little interest or juice to them how a record came to be. If, for example, you tell them how Berry Gordy didn't want to release "What's Going On" by Marvin Gaye, or that Sly Stone covered "Que Sera Sera" because the papers thought he was loving Doris Day up, their eyes tend to glaze over and their minds wander of as if they had somewhere better to be.

Gals never check for such details but they certainly move in other mysterious ways which is why I was now bound Westward Ho, to seek urgent advice on the latest development in Sandra's life.

To be sure, I much prefer tube travel to any other and the reasons for my preference are many. It is easily the quickest way, barring delays and the like, to scoot around town, allowing you to travel to all points with relatively ease.

On the tube you have time to get up to all kinds of things that you put off at home, such as reading or thinking or even listening to tunes on your walkman, and before you know it, there, you've arrived at your destination.

I know that most prefer cars but I have seen too many of my links go from happy to mad within five minutes of driving in this city, with its crumbling roads, huge traffic jams and Mad Max drivers, that I wish to steer clear of such distress.

Of course, the tube is not perfect by any stretch of the HQ and it's even worse come the rush hour p.m. and the people cram in, just as they had to that morning, their exhausted pissed off faces as eloquent a testimony to the cruel nature of work as anything else.

Yet come the weekend it's slightly different because then most of them are travelling for pleasure and so I wasn't too surprised, as I pulled out Sam Selvon's "The Lonely Londoners," to hear a loud West Country accent assail me with an, "Easy Mr.DJ man, how's your percentage of life?" and realised that it was none other than Sammy The Foot who was addressing me.

This is a character who I am on speaking terms with, such as I am with The Sherrif, Stinga or Jasmine, through my position at The Unity Club, and whose yard is in close proximity to mine.

Sammy The Foot frequents The Unity but the location of most of our meetings has been at clubs where jazz is the only music played and which always attracts a small but dedicated crowd who are normally some of the best movers in town.

Sammy The Foot is no exception, a jazz dancer of real excellence, capable of busting the kind of athletic and gracious moves that make you ashamed to be within ten yards of him on the dancefloor as he goes into his routine.

When Sammy The Foot and his comrades, some of whom come from as far as Manchester to indulge in their passion, take to the floor, you know it is time to discreetly retire because that space is his true home and although he and his friends never flash it in a look-at-me-I'm-so-great manner, it is still best to simply pull back and watch, rather than compete in any way.

Furthermore, such is Sammy's love of jazz and dance, that his gears are all old style such as you see in fading pictures of various jazz musicians and their audience, his public attire often consisting of such items as large caps, zoot suits and brown and white spats, all of which give you the impression that Sammy just left The Cotton Club in Harlem and waltzed into the present. Today was no exception with Sammy sporting an eye catching grey pin striped baggy suit, a small flower in the left lapel of his double breasted jacket, white shirt and flowered tie, a walking stick and two tone shoes. On his head, tipped at an angle, was a large trilby. Sammy looked every bit the celebrity that he aspired to be and this desire, so legend had it, was first nurtured in him many years ago when he made his first TV appearance, albeit unwittingly, as a little kiddiwink.

The story has it that Sammy was but seven years old when a general election was called and the local Conservative MP returned to Sammy's home base of Yeovil for the first time in years, a camera crew in tow with which to capture him on the campaign trail routine of kissing bambinos, cuddling old folk and blaming everyone but himself and his party for society's ills. Sammy's folks are Nigerians and you don't get too many of them to the pound in the British countryside. In fact, you don't get any so when the aspiring MP spotted Sammy and his mum out and about, innocently walking the High Street to get the shopping, he saw a unique chance to do something for race relations in this country.

"Hello, young man," the MP boomed, picking up Sammy much to his astonishment, "what part of the world were you born in?" The camera zoomed in expectantly on a bewildered Sammy and the old smiling politico who, no doubt, was expecting the name of some far off exotic country that the British had "civilized" not so long ago to drop from Sammy's lips.

"Yeovil," Sammy said. "I come from Yeovil."

The MP, momentarily stunned and bewildered, froze and then quickly put down Sammy saying, with a smile as transparent as water, "Yes, of course you are. Now whose this pretty little girl over here?" and marched off, praying no one noticed his burning cheeks of embarassment.

The whole sorry incident was briefly shown on TV that night but with the commentator's voice running over the film so all you saw was the MP cuddling Sammy and you never heard his words. Through it, Sammy became something of a cause celebre in his hometown, with all the kids at his school treating him as a major figure, "because he was on telly," until three weeks later the MP was returned to Parliament with an increased majority and everyone forgot the incident and got on with their lives. No doubt the bug of holding centre stage had been planted in the young one from that point on because whenever you saw him you couldn't help but be overwhelmed by his ability to walk in to any public place and have everything revolve around him and not vice versa, which is how it runs for the majority.

"Easy Sammy," I said, putting away my book, "how goes it?"

"Not too well Mr. DJ man," he replied, sitting down next to me and smiling ever so graciously at the lady opposite who was obviously taken with his attire and demeanour.

"The Loved One is on my case again."

"Trouble with your gal?"

"She tells me that I pay more attention to dancing than I do her and soon she will walk if I do not change my ways." He shrugged his shoulders.

"But she'll come round. I knows it."

What's fascinating about Sammy is that the man's true vocation is not really dancing, although God knows he is a right little Nureyev when he gets going, but it is the art of acting that he has truly mastered. This is his main strength and the reason for my take on him came one night when, in an unguarded moment, he led me through the rhyme and reasons of his life. When Sammy quit Yeovil in his teens, the only offer of a job being at the helicopter factory, he arrived in the Capital knowing neither friend or foe, a major problem for a lot of faces who descend from the hinterlands looking to escape the dull local action of pubs, fights, marriage, mortgage, kids and death. In Sammy The Foot's case, the idea of hosting a TV show had grabbed him the strongest, a wish no doubt stemming from the infamous MP incident and with that view in mind, Sammy quit home and made for the Capital.

Shocked and troubled at first by the impersonal nature of this city, Sammy spent his first few months in a miserable bedsit, signing on and aimlessly wandering around town looking for a friendly face, going to bed at night not a little scared, until one day it dawned on him that if London was not to come to Sammy, why then, he must go to London and grab it by the scruff of the neck. Jazz music being his first love, a condition brought about by his mother's pre-occupation with be-bop, Sammy sought out the underground jazz clubs and spent hours leaning against a wall, memorising the moves he witnessed on the dancefloor. Nighttime, at home, he would, much to the annoyance of the neighbour below him, practise these moves for hours on end whilst during the day he scoured the Oxfam shops for suitable gears, knowing full well that when he made his entrance into the life, his eccentric gears style would instantly set him apart. He would also, he recognised, have to hide that part of his nature which was shy and retiring so that he would always exhude poise and confidence, qualities that everyone is instantly attracted to if only because they wish some of it to rub off on themselves. Come the day that Sammy The Foot took to the dancefloor, it was with such style and grace that within weeks people were checking for this strangely dressed but brilliant mover and gravitating towards him. Sammy The Foot played his part, coming on mysterious, whetting people's appetites and all the time building up contacts. In no time at all, he had secured a relationship with a well off gal from the Surrey countryside and moved in with her but his constant drive towards fame meant that he spent a lot of time "at work," as he called his lengthy stay in club after club, and that had started to bug out his lady.

"She thinks I should be at home with her every night," he explained to me as we hurtled down the dark tunnel, the tube rocking from side to side, "but how am I to meet people if I don't make the rounds. You tell me."

I had no answer to his question and even if I had I wouldn't have spilt it because ten times out of ten it is never wise to get involved in a couple's runnings for the partner in distress only wants to hear what they want to hear, and no matter what you say or reason, their heart, not their head will guide them each and every time. As the heart has no use for reason, the only time to give forth your opinion is if your closest link comes to you for advice or wisdom and you state all of the above. Otherwise it is best to take the fifth on the grounds that you may incriminate yourself and a friendship, and as nothing is worth that, I changed the talk.

"You out and about last night, Sammy?"

"That is exactly my point," he said, determined to take the weight off his shoulders by talking it through.

"Last night, there was an all nighter going off down Hammersmith way. I inform my lady that I will be present and correct and that I would very much like her to accompany me. She tells me, that she is sick of my stepping out, that I am just using her for cashola purposes and that if I do not stay in and miss the jam then we are finished. I tell her sure, babe. If that's what you want. But first I must go out and buy some cigarettes. Of course, once I am in the night air the bug bites me, so I figure I'll just slip over to the dance, spend half an hour at best and then return home.

"I reach the club and before I know it I am being approached by two TV people who are wishing to make a film about the jazz scene. We exchange numbers and I am to go and see them next week."

"That's great Sammy."

"Not for my lady it isn't. When I got home I tell her of my great fortune and that everything will be alright. She told me, "really". Then went back to sleep."

"So where are you heading for now."

"Blackpool."

"Blackpool?"

"Yes indeed. I am off to munch on rock and see the famous lights."

"And," I said cottoning on, "to attend the Jazz weekender that is going off there."

"Yes but look, if you see my gal you haven't seen me, okay? I am considering going invisible over the next few days just to get my head into shape over this sorry state of affairs."

"Sammy, none of my business but you have been with your gal longtime and you shouldn't distress her too much. At least bell her."

"Maybe," he said with a shrug and tossing a sly wink at the woman opposite who, having followed our every word with great indiscretion, promptly turned red and looked away, "and maybe not. I know what you're saying but she has to learn that I don't rush around for just my benefit but hers as well. If she can't see that, why then, what can she see?"

The train pulled into Kings Cross and Sammy jumped up. "Gotta slide, this is my stop. Go well, Mr. DJ man and no whispering in the corridors. I'll check you at The Unity soon. Know what I mean and mean what I know? Laters."

"Laters, Sammy."

No doubt about it, our brief conflab had been a pleasant diversion from my own woes and worries but pondering on Sammy The Foot's relationship got my HQ whirring away and soon I was relating it all back to my present unhealthy condition and wondering what would have happened if I and the First Lady had kept it together, and where would I be now, and what would I be doing, and all those other pointless notions that you fall into thinking about when self pity wells up and spreads itself inside of you.

I should explain here something about this teenage trauma which haunts me so and which kicked off, back in the days of my schooltime, and introduce to you one Miss Tuesday Driver, First

Sweetheart of my life, a cool, collected woman who had my heart flipping this way and that for all the time I knew her. Tuesday always was and always will be ten steps ahead of everyone else, walking the paths no one else dared to with a determined self belief in herself that rubbed everybody up the wrong way. She came to my attention when her and her mother, the father has passed away at an early age, moved to London and she enrolled at my school just as the fourth year was fading out. I didn't even notice her presence in our class until the afternoon, one of those hot sticky days where all you could do was gaze out of the window and wish you were miles away, drifting away on a barge that gently carried you up and down the gentle Thames, sunning yourself up, quenching thirst, listening to music, and then suddenly realising that it wasn't the bees that you could hear droning around and about you but the relentlessly dull words of the ancient, white haired history teacher that stood before you, delivering the same lecture that he had given all his life to, as far as he was concerned, the same pupils but with their names changed. Just as he was finishing off some business about Roundheads and Cavaliers, there was the sound, from the back of the room a chair scraping against the floor.

"Excuse me sir," came a female and unfamiliar to me voice, "I don't mean to be rude but surely in the period that you are talking about, Cromwell was responsible for launching an invasion of Ireland, the consequences of which are still us with now as we see on our TV's most nights."

There was a brief, stunned silence. Then a few giggles and then, before the teacher could muster a reply, one of the lads shouted out, "yes sir, what about Cromwell and the paddies!" Half the class cracked into laughter and Miss Tuesday Driver simply collected up her books and majestically walked out. "Where on earth do you think you're going?" the History Man demanded but Tuesday was out of the door before his words could even reach her. She turned up for class the next morning, after everyone had seen her emerging tight lipped from the Head's office, by which time I was head over heels and the boys were all calling her Maggie, after our glorious PM. Then and there I prepared to move everything in sight to win her over, a task made predictably easier by the aforementioned caveman types running a mile everytime she came into view. At that point in my life I was consumed with shyness when it came to gals and so when, that very weekend, I bumped into her at a record fair, my heart skipped a double beat. Uno, because she was standing right beside me flicking through the seven inch singles laid out on a table, and I had never been this close to her, and due, because women are a rare sight at such functions as they are at those antiquated men only clubs for retired bankers (rhyme it) and colonels, the sort you read about with increasing incredulity in those posh magazines they leave out for you at the local surgery. Tuesday seemed lost in her mission and so when I ventured a brief, "Hi, how you doing?" it was as if I had just awoken her from some trance. She looked at me questioningly until she was able to fit the face and then gave me a small nod of recognition.

"Oh, it's you," she said as if making an important discovery. "It's a bit pricey here, isn't it?"

"What are you looking for?"

"Girl soul."

"As opposed to boy soul."

"Definitely. Women sing it better than men. They've got more to lose and you can hear it."

I was intrigued by her outlook just as I was by her appearance which consisted of a smart white raincoat, a small black woolen hat that rested on the back of her head and tried to stem the long black hair that fell inexplorably down her back, black Sta-prest looking trousers and a pair of penny loafers.

She had small, piercing blue eyes, a nose that turned up ever so slightly and a wide mouth that always gave the impression that she was brooding about something.

"Is there anywhere you can get a coffee around here?" she suddenly asked.

"There's a place across the road," I replied.

"Good."

Tuesday began to walk off and then turned back to me, myself and I, standing quite transfixed. "Coming?" she said with a smile. "I won't bite."

Over the cappuccino swing, Tuesday told me of her background, growing up in South Ireland amidst beautiful countryside and living the village life. When her father suffered his second heart attack and passed from this earth to the next, the mother, distraught and unable to live with the memories, moved to London in search of a new land. Tuesday was 14 years old.

"My father knew he was weak physically and so from an early age he prepared me for his passing. He talked to me about it and said I had nothing to fear and not to worry or grieve over him as he was going onto a much better place where we would eventually meet up again. I believed him. I still do."

Tuesday (so christened because that was the day of her arrival) and her mother moved in with friends first, and then a distant uncle let them rent one of his properties, a run down house that they were doing up in return for rent, and as this was down the way from my school, that's where she had landed. When I unravelled my story, born and bred in London, P&M still together, happy childhood, it sounded, next to her fable of loss and journey, quite commonplace. Yet Tuesday listened to my particulars as if I was relating the most exciting story in the world and I found myself gladly falling further into her universe. I asked her out. She blushed just a touch and said, "sure, why not? But what ever will your friends say about you being seen with Maggie, eh?"

"That," I replied, "is of no interest to me."

Even so, under her insistence, we kept our liaisons something of a secret from the Pleb Patrol that stalked my school and, six months later, on a night etched forever in my HQ, we lost our virginities to one another in a small hotel pad, room 77, that we both saved up to hire. The one incident that I will never forget from that night happened when, so overcome by the nervous excitement of it all, the booking in under different names and the growing realisation that what I had dreamt about every night for what seemed like forever, was actually going to happen, I rushed everything and finished way too early.

Turning my head away from her in burning shame, I crumbled against her body waiting and wishing for the sheets we lay on to wrap themselves around me and whisk me up and away to anywhere but this room. But that gal of mine had a real heart. She simply lifted up her hand, placed it on my head and stroked my hair.

And then she said, "I'm so glad that it was you. It was lovely."

Tuesday taught me many things in the following months that I still abide by, such as always go with your feelings, whatever the cost, and never be scared, for no matter how bad things are there is always the way through. It explained why, as soon as they could, the school let Tuesday go and she happily made for the exit, strong in the knowledge that no matter what the odds she would always pull through. I dug that gal big time and there was nothing else to tell me differently until that nightmare evening when my heart took a blow that it is only now just recovering from.

I had gone to pick up Tuesday for an evening of cinema and cappuccino and so could not understand why, when I reached their house, all the lights were off and no-one was in. I rang the bell repeatedly and even chucked a couple of small pebbles at the window. Nothing doing. I went home and awaited her call. For two days there was nothing but big silence. Worried now that some great misfortune had overtaken them, I went back to their abode that afternoon.

When I reached, the sight of some builders erecting their scaffolding at the front of the house caused my heart to sink. Stopping one of them I asked him his business.

"We're turning the house into flats," is all he would say.

"What about the people who lived here?" I anxiously asked.

"What about them?" he replied, and walked off. I stood there gazing at the scene in complete disbelief, utterly confused and not knowing what I was to do. A week later, seven restless nights of frustration and heartache, a letter, addressed to me, came through the post. It simply read, "Sorry but we had to move. There was nothing I could do. Please take good care of yourself. I will always care for you. T."

To this day, I still have no clear idea of what happened except that the ground was cruelly taken from under my feet and I was pushed hard into a bottomless pit of despair and anger. Ah, let's drop it for it still vexes me to think about it. Suffice to say, Tuesday's masterful Houdini act left my HQ completely haywire over the whole guys and gals programme, and it was just as I was coming to that I met Sandra. As you can no doubt pinpoint, my clock was still set to Tuesday time and so I refused to see Sandra in any other light than that of the most basic. Naturally, as far as Sandra was concerned, this was not too much to her liking. For women, the act itself is rarely enough. If they are to be intimate with their bodies then it's usually a two to one odds on fave that there should also be an intimacy of the mind and heart. It is rare, I reckon, that a woman can walk away time and time again from a close encounter of the flesh and be satisfied with that and that alone. Since we are vamping on the subject, it should also be made clear that for a lot of guys such notions never come into play if only because John Thomas does not understand these ways and, what's more, has shown little inclination to learn this lingo.

Most of the time it's as if gals like to build bridges which the guys then exert a lot of their time refusing to cross, all the time thinking, what will it gain me to lose freedom for the chores of responsibility. This scenario is not helped by the fact that gals become women far faster than guys become men and so there will always be a time difference between the two, like an athlete in a relay race waiting anxiously for the rest of their lives for the baton to be passed on. I ascended the Oxford Circus escalator and was up into the West End sunshine which beat down upon the masses rushing here, there and everywhere.

To be honest I would like to give you the exact location of my meet with the Brother P. but find myself unable to do so because our regular haunt, a coffee spot we always use, is yet to be dicsovered and we wish to keep it clear from unsavoury characters and, no offence to your good self, but you never know who is looking in these days. Let me just say that Papa Supino's is to be located in the deepest part of the West End and is run by an Italian family that we are inordinately fond of primarily because of their very cool way of letting us sit for hours and hours chewing the fat at one of their tables, whilst only ordering cappuccinos. The Brother P. and I are also, it must be stated, drawn to them on a deeper level and that has much to do with the way that the whole family, barring their son Paolo, are totally at ease with themselves, exhuding a contentment with life and, consequently, they display their emotions far easier than a lot of the tight lipped and repressed British, a condition that even I, born and raised in such an atmosphere, find impossible to escape.

For the example, if something upsets Papa, and that's usually his son's ambition to turn professional as a footballer and not takeover the family business, then Papa doesn't care one iota whose around to see him let off. In his loud, native language, he screams and curses until he reaches such a crescendo that anyone entering the cafe at that precise moment would probably believe that a murder had just taken place, or some similar disaster, which is when Marissa, his wife and best friend intervenes, and talks him down with all the skill of a diplomat.

Equally, if good fortune comes his way, such as his team Napoli winning some big game, then you will no doubt witness Papa singing loudly and urging his wife to dance around the tables and chairs, Papa is of medium height and looks at you with eyes that might have come straight off Bambi thus giving him, despite all his noise and bluff, a real little boy lost look. He has a largish nose, hair that has turned from black to grey and full red cheeks. His longtime companion in life, Marissa, is still something of a stunna. Much to the envy of her friends back in Italia, I should imagine, she has kept her figure whilst in her face, you can clearly see the exceptional beauty that surely must have turned many a head in the streets. Her eyes are jet black and these are set off even further by her delicate porcelain cheeks which accentuate even further their mood of both sadness and joy. She is also a kind, wise woman genuinely interested in all you have to say, often sitting down, if there is no immediate work to be done, for a pow wow that is always warm hearted. As I entered the cafe, she was the first to greet me as I ordered two capos and took my fave seat by the window, a position that allows me, myself and I to gaze upon the Capital's citizens whilst daydreaming away the hour. As soon as she clocked me Marissa knew something was up for I lack Sammy The Foot's immense acting ability and can never create disguises.

After placing the coffees in front of me, she touched my arm, and said, "You look a little pale today. Are you feeling alright? Perhaps you have a cold coming."

"No, no, no. I'm cool. Everything is fine. I'm just waiting for my friend."

Marissa looked at me briefly with slight bemusement and moved off to the counter to help Papa prepare the sandwiches for the lunchtime rush, which, it being Saturday, would not be as hectic as the weekday.

Papa's is actually a small joint and looks more like a take away operation than anything else for there are only a few chairs and tables to sit at and it is normally the long queues of bored office workers that stretch out onto the pavement, their glazed eyes reflecting the tedium of their work, that enables the Supinos to make cashola.

I had not waited too long before Brother P. reached and was entering the cafe decked out immaculately in brown brogues, white and brown dog tooth strides, a white button down collar and a green suede jacket. A sight for sore eyes, indeed. He came over and rested his hand lightly on my shoulder and asked, "Cool?" before turning and saluting the Supinos and then coming to rest by sitting down in front of me.

"This earth gets warmer by the day," he said with a slight nod to outside, "and that is not good news. It's too hot for this time of the year. In winter it has to get cold so that things die and can be reborn."

"Tell me about it," I replied. "Only a jacket and shirt today."

Brother P. took a sip of his capo and sized me down.

"So, what's up," he said stirring his chocolate into the coffee and getting straight to the reason for this hastily convened meet.

"It's a heavy one," I warned him, "very heavy. I still can't believe what has just gone down."

Brother P. reached inside his shirt pocket and removed a pack of Du Marier cigs and with smoke now issuing forth from our mouths and noses, I began my unhappy fable.

"You know that chick Sandra I've been checking these past few months."

"Jill's friend. The one with the legs."

"Exactly. She's pregnant."

Brother P. didn't blink.

"Is it yours?"

"I don't know. She says it is but I am not with her every minute of the day so what do I know? She could be pulling a fast one but somehow I don't think so. But then who is to say?"

"Exactly," said Brother P., he himself being quite averse to partnerships of most shadings except for family and a very few close links, such as myself. He was not one to be checking gals every minute of the day and often referred me, when we hit upon the subject, to a cab driver he had once found himself in deep concentration with some years ago and whose story had truly touched and influenced his own runnings.

The driver, revealed his age as around the 50 mark whilst in the process of talking with obvious love and affectation about his 12 year old daughter. Putting two against two, Brother P. came up with four and wondered out aloud why the man had waited so long to sow seed.

"Ah," said the driver, "don't get me wrong. I have loved women all my life. To me they are the finest race on this earth I have always thought this and so I have also ran around with a lot of them. Much better fun than hanging out at the bar with the men, I can say. I had a great time but as I went into my 20s and especially into my 30s, everyone started getting on my case about getting married. You must get married, they said, life is not complete without it. If you're worried that you can not carry on as before, you can always take a mistress. Everyone else does in Trinidad.

"They didn't seem to realise that the reason for my big reluctance was very simple. I hadn't met anyone. I liked very much all the women I hung out with but I never loved them in the way that you must love someone if you are to spend the rest of your days with them. Now, of course, that got everybody's goat up. Family, friends, even the local priest, all of them like a chorus line in my ear singing, you have to marry, you have to marry.

"I just took my time because I knew that one day I would meet someone and if I didn't what was the point of complaining? That was my roll of the dice. Simple as that. Sure enough, two weeks after my 40th birthday, I met a Spanish lady and the minute I saw her and she me, that was it. Six months later we were married and now I have four children, I have given up all my ladies and I have never been happier."

Brother P. loved that story because it told him one vital thing - never compromise your instincts. Believe in them and they will always see you through. This then was his outlook on it all and so, when it came to female company, the Brother P. moved in mysterious circles and silence and although I was one of the few to be privy to his dealings on this front, I always felt that he kept something back from me and never came through with the full melody.

"I really don't know what to do about this one," I told the Brother P., draining off the capo and horrified at the tone of pleading I heard in my voice. "I can't become a father. It's ridiculous."

"If you don't mind me saying, the first thing to do is not worry yourself up until you have ascertained it's your kiddiwink. As you say, you don't know. Otherwise, you'll sink into that spliff and Nina Simone on the turntable all day long and worry yourself to death when there's no need."

"I know a chick," Brother P, continued, "who has had dealings with Sandra before. I'll see what the score is. She maybe bluffing or testing you out. You going to meet her soon?"

"Monday. Bloody Monday."

"Then before you see her we'll try and sort out what the plot really is. Okay?"

"Sure."

Then Brother P. dropped the clanger.

"There's no way you want this baby, right?"

"Easy, P."

"I'm serious. It might be good for you," he said with a slight raising of the eyebrows.

"Oh, you think so, do you," I challenged. "I've just started at The Unity and I need to keep that job down. Once I've shelled out for my expenses there's not exactly a lot left and so what do you suggest I do. Get a nine to five and come home to a woman I hardly know every night?"

"You don't have to do that. Just have the child. You stay in your place. The kiddiwink goes to Sandra's and you go visit every so often."

"Yeah, alright P. That simple. Right?"

"Most things in life are simple. Except people always have to complicate. We've spoken about this before. 2,000 years on this planet and we still haven't figured out how to wash, clothe and feed everyone. Same with you. It's not the disaster you think it is. There is always a way around things, the trick is to find that way. But it exists and if you think it doesn't then that only means you haven't seen it."

"Look Mr. Fix It, I have already told you on many an occasion that when I bring kiddwinks of my own into this world I fully intend it to be with the woman I am staying with for the rest of my life. It may have escaped your attention but I am hardly head over with the ever so lovely Miss Sandra. Seen? I am not your cousin."

As you can check, sometimes my tongue slips a bit nasty as it had just done with that reference to one of Brother P.'s family numbers, a truly mad second cousin who, in his infinite wisdom had purchased, from God knows where, one of those old style crowns that you always see the dead Kings and Queens of England sporting in history book pictures.

Something of a Royalist, he had locked away the crown in his wardrobe, intending, when the time was right to place this gleaming item on the head of his blushing and beautiful bride. For years the crown gathered dust as the would be King searched the land for his intended until one day the cheerful news rang out from his yard. Cousin Ernie had found his Princess. The Crown would be used. Happy as the man who has discovered oil, the crowning, or should I say the wedding, took place one bright Saturday afternoon in Chelsea although Cousin Ernie, by all accounts, looked extremely tense and unhappy come his great day. Putting his demeanour down to nerves, everyone was in great mood as the ceremony took place and Ernie crowned his princess amidst much happiness. All and sundry then retired to the reception room for speeches, champagne and the whole caboodle.

It was there they heard the bride, a blushing beauty if ever there was one, make a speech to the effect that yes, this was indeed the happiest day of her life and that in Ernie she had found everything that she was searching for, and she was sure they would be so happy, and thank you all very much for coming. The best man then rose and and launched into one about the old days, him and Ernie meeting up and hitting it off, moving to Britain and looking out for each other as they struggled to make ends meet, and the less said about that incident with a bottle of rum and a copper the better, and, now here he was, all married up with a wonderful woman and why, it even brought tears to his eyes, and with a slap on the back, they all rose to toast bride and groom. After that, Cousin Ernie then stood up with a very serious expression on his face. It was he said a very special occasion and his heart had indeed been moved by all these folk coming out today, but it was with special gratitude that he looked upon both his best man and his wife, if only because a week ago he found out that they had been sleeping with each other behind his back for the last month. Uproar and recrimination quickly ensued with the two families, who had been warm and nice together all day, starting to exchange punches and insults, with tables being turned over, plates, cups and glasses smashing to the floor, until one of the younger boys pulled out a knife and everyone went screaming out into the street. When asked why, after this horrific discovery, he had gone ahead with the marriage, Cousin Ernie simply replied, "to get my own back. She's still legally my wife." Then he kicked his crown across the floor and walked out a broken man. That night the wife told him she was pregnant. By him. They would stay together. They would have to. For the children. Which is all very honourable, no doubt about it, but I was not about to go the same way with Miss Sandra, no sir, and that's what I was trying to tell the Brother P.

"It's funny about children," Brother P. observed, going off on one of his tangents as he is wont to do when his HQ warms up, and now staring out of the window.

"The odd one out at my school was this kid who lived in the local children's home. Nowadays, I bet it's the kid with the P&M still together whose the strange one."

Papa's voice suddenly boomed out from behind the counter. "Eh boys, you want some more coffee? A little cake and a sandwich maybe. Both of you should eat more. You're like two scarecrows. One day I'll put you in a field so you can scare the birds away, eh Marissa?"

"Leave them alone. They're not doing any harm."

"You want another capo?" Brother P. offered.

I shook my head in a manner that was meant to show how unconcerned I was but it must have come out as a miserable defeated gesture for Brother P. said, "You'll have to let time clear the clouds for you on this one. There's no other way.. Anything could happen. You just don't know."

"Yeah?" I replied, totally unconvinced that any good could ever come of the situation unfolding before me, "that's exactly what's bugging me out. Let's pay and split."

The two of us rose and went to hand over cashola to the boss.

"I'll get these," Brother P. offered, digging deep into his pocket. "Papa," he said, "how much I owe?"

"Two pounds but as it's you, then let's just say two pounds."

"How, by the way, is your team Napoli? Prospering?"

Above Papa and the Gaggia machine a huge poster of that chunky ball of muscle and pure skills known as Maradona, stared indolently down at us, the right hand clutching a ball to his hip (the same one he used to push the ball into the England net back in '86 and left a nation gasping about cheating foreigners, everyone conveniently forgetting his tremendous second goal, 15 minutes later, when he picked the ball up on the half way line, left four defenders choking on his dust and scored), the face full of arrogance.

The mention of Maradona was normally the cue for Papa to go into one about his beloved Napoli team but these days the subject of the world's greatest sport was a touchy one.

"Ah, football," he said, with great seriousness, "only the lucky ones make it. The rest of us have to work the hours God sends us and not fill our heads with nonsense, thinking you can become something that you are not."

Papa was not talking about Napoli, in fact he wasn't even talking to us, but to his absent son Paolo and as the argument between them was now further away than ever before from being resolved, deep frustration was creeping into his everyday moods.

Brother P. nodded up to the poster.

"Maradona had to start somewhere. In the streets by the look of him."

Papa gave out a snort of disgust.

"There is only one Maradona, one Pele, one Gary Lineker," is all he would say and it dawned on me, myself and I that this must be the worst bit of a father's job, when despite all the knowledge and experience that you have gathered up over the years with which to guide and protect your own children, they refuse to listen to you but, like everyone in those teen times, would actually prefer that you were not there.

"Where are you off to now, boys?" Marissa asked before Papa could work up a steam of head and truly go into one in the manner that I have described before.

"We are off to check some new records," Brother P. replied.

"Ah, that's nice. I like music."

It was the smart move on my compadre's behalf because if there was one thing guaranteed to ward off at least some of my troubled spirits it had to be my dear friend music, and so we made with the ciao's ciao's and headed off to The Vinyl Market, a shop I often frequent when on the prowl for new tunes.

For a Saturday morning the shop, when we reached, was surprisingly quiet which, I have to say, was something of a bonus for it meant that I got first crack at all the new releases before my contemporaries but Dillon, the only assistant who had managed to reach his post that morning by the look of things, was about to let me down on that score.

"Delivery has been held up until this afternoon," he nonchantly told myself and my companion, as he donned his headphones for a day of manning the shop's dex, playing new tunes and old to customers, "apparently there's been some trouble at the airport."

Now, the one thing that has to be said in Dillon's favour, and the reason that I have time for him, is that he does not follow the suit of so many other record shop numbers and try and pull a fast one on you by playing new tunes at the highest decibel there is, thus giving a false impression of its real worth.

Back in the days, I was forever getting home and discovering that what had just sounded so brilliant in the shop an hour before, was actually, when you played it at home, all excited up, just another run of the mill tune. Dillon didn't deal in such bad business which is why I frequented his premises because you get a little tired of feeling duped by people with smiling faces and an eye on your pocket.

"Come back then. Nicky will be in soon and she might have some new tunes downstairs."

In the shop's basement, Nicky looked after the rap and swingbeat tunes and this, incidentally, was where I first met Dillon before he was promoted upstairs, following a St. Paul'like conversion to the varied delights of House music, and it was here, I had noticed over my last few visits, that more and more people had started to congregate.

"Have you heard about this club tonight over Southside?"

Dillon enquired, pulling out a tune from its wrapper.

"It's at some gym or other. Should be good, you know." He picked up one of the many flyers that decorate the counter and handed it over. I scanned the card, which had a smiley face printed in the top hand corner and all the facts and figures written beneath it, and then handed it back to Dillon, which was when I noticed the dark circles under his eyes, the tight red veins on his forehead and the overall glazed nature of his face.

To be straight, Dillon has always come on to Brother P. and I as a serious space cadet, a man not averse to tampering with his brain cells on a regular basis. His cheeks are pale and sinking, and his actual eyes, when he brushes his long brown fringe of hair out of them, have a slightly manic hunted look about them. It was no shocker, then, that Dillon was the first bod I heard talking about the drug ecstasy, an item he referred to by its street name.

"You can get 'E' down there, you know," he said, placing the tune on the dex, although such info is of no use to either myself or Brother P. as we never indulge on the chemical trip, herb and brew being our favoured method of relaxing.

"It's good, man," continued Dillon, "I had one last night it was great." He mixed in the tune and that unmistakeable, basic House beat came thudding through the speakers. The tune being played was obviously a bit•of a hit with Dillon because within seconds he was jerking his body and moving his arms in a style that was both weird and unfunky. I had just seen the future and I didn't know it. With the music up so loud that you could hardly hear yourself parlare, Brother P. and I needed no more encouragement and, with a slight nod of the heads, we made for the exit sign, signalling our departure with sign language.

"Jesus," said Brother P. as we hit the pavement and put some serious space between ourselves and Dillon, "did you see his eyes? I don't think he's landed since take off last night."

"You're right on that one," I replied, "although to be honest, I wouldn't mind checking out that club he was on about. Someone else was on about it last week. You up for it?"

"Maybe," came the reply which was typical of Brother P. for he is a man who never likes to plan too far ahead and rarely decides to visit a club until at least an hour after it has kicked off.

"Let's go Portobello," he said. "There's a jacket I've had put aside and I want to bag it before anyone else," and with that mission in mind, we journeyed to West London, an area in which both poor and rich live within breathing space of each other, and such a combination in any town, makes for a fascinating spectacle.

Portobello Market, as expected, was crammed when we reached and, as ever, it was difficult to negotiate past all the citizens and keep a tab on my companion. There was noise all around us as rap, reggae and funk music came blasting out of ghetto blasters, smashing into each other in mid air to create glorious sonic explosions over our heads.

Kiddiwinks appeared from nowhere and ran into your legs whilst people either jostled to get past or suddenly stopped right in front of you to examine an item, thus causing you to bump, like a dodgem car, into their backs. The whole area was full of life and colour and a great place to be in the City sunshine for you were often surrounded by cats of your own age or faces you knew from the clubs which you acknowledged with discreet nods of the head, here, there and everywhere.

On the actual stalls, a colourful collection of bohemians, rastas, hustlers, students, artists, old timers, jack the lads, and the unemployed tried to move their wares, shouting the odds for all to hear, but the Brother P. cut through them like a shark intent on its victim, walking straight and fast towards an old boy who specialised in period clothing. He had only just put up shop but, not having done his homework, underpriced his goodies and Brother P. wanted to get to him before others cottoned onto his mistake or, worse still, picked up on the red and black striped, three button jacket, complete with epaulets, that Brother P. had spotted the day before and, not having the correct cashola on him, persuaded to have put by for him whilst he raised the neccesary loot, and no questions asked. Reaching the stall, the old boy revealed that he had not gone back on his promise and produced the item in question.

"What do you think?" asked the Brother P. as he examined it and then tried it on.

"Why, you will be the hit of the ball," I replied.

Pleased with the analysis, Brother P. spent the next three minutes studying the effect of the jacket on him in front of a fading mirror as if he was not really sure of its place in his wardrobe but all the time playing the old boy along with pleasant humour until a deal had been struck and there were smiles all round.

"Foodage time," I suggested as Brother P. proudly placed the jacket under his arm and nodded his agreement.

The Portobello Cafe is a small West Indian joint where it takes ages to get your order dealt up but once it arrives and you take a bite, your impatience suddenly disappears as the flavour flav of the food invades your mouth.

As we strolled in, I heard a soft voice from one of the tables beside me, say, "ah ah," and knew that it could only be Daddy Cecil, a serious young dude whose mocking humour had been devised for no other purpose than to casually and purposefully wound you.

"Why, it's the I Spy boys in the flesh," he said with an engaging grin for this was Daddy Cecil's nickname for us and the only acquaintance we knew to make a song and dance about the fact that Brother P. and I carry different skin colours, a trait of Daddy Cecil's that is derived from his ambition in life to become the first British black leader to lead his people into total seperation from the white man.

Daddy Cecil had adopted the Muslim faith many crescent moons ago and had put his all behind the teachings and guidance of Minister Louis Farrakhan, the leader of America's Nation Of Islam, whose audio and video tapes Daddy Cecil studied, examined and memorised, a member of his family in New York shipping over a new batch every three months or so.

When the tapes arrived, Daddy Cecil would invite his posse over to his yard for study time and late into the night they would parlare about such items as the white man as the devil, how Ethiopia was the cradle of civilization and not Greece, the place of the black woman in society, the commercialisation of black music by the music industry, the representation of blacks within cinema, and a hundred other subjects, with constant reference being made to the works of people such as Marcus Garvey, Patrice Lamumba, Stokely Carmichael, Elijah Muhammad, Malcolm X. and up to date cats such as the Reverend Al Sharpton. Daddy Cecil and the boys dressed downstyle but with a definite Afro-centric flavour, proudly sporting their African pendants, beads and Muslim hats to make their position in public loud and clear, and although there were few numbers in their team, Daddy Cecil's undoubted charisma and passing resemblance to a young Muhammad Ali, marked him out as numero uno in his outfit.

On the occasions that I had parlared with him, Daddy Cecil always adopted a patronising attitude, so I never gave him trust, nor did my closest companion, Brother P., who found his arguments on racism clear and correct but his proposed solution totally unrealistic and, in some ways, slightly humorous.

He told me, "boy, us Carribean people have enough trouble getting along with each other, let alone anybody else."

What the Brother P. had hit upon was truer than true and not just confined to his people. Many was the time that Papa, over a quick capo in the afternoon break, would lament about the Northern Italians who always dissed his people in the South, or, indeed, take this fair land with its North/South bickering running up and down its spine, and this amongst people of the same hue and complexion. All I knew is that it always suits someone somewhere to have the people at each other's throats and exploit their tribal allegiances over the most dumbest of arguments and, on top of that, you can't help but notice how people love to box up and label, like a birthday present, everything in this world just so that they can make sense of it all and know where they stand.

"So what's up, I Spy boys?"

"Cool, man."

"Safe."

"Sit, have a drink. Tell me how things are," Daddy Cecil requested although he had addressed all his wordage to Brother P. and hardly glanced at me, although we knew each other from around the clubs.

"They allowing you to make a buck?" he asked the Brother P. as we pulled out chairs to the table.

"I allow for myself," came the reply.

"Good, good, I am glad to hear it. I too am getting by but, boy, it's a struggle. Last night, I had the posse over at my yard and we spoke deep into the night until suddenly there was a knock at the door and the police were there. Some white neighbour had rung them to complain about noise."

He kissed his teeth in disgust. "We're living in a fascist state and no one gives a shit about it."

The fact of the matter was that everytime Daddy C. had cause to use the word white, it was like putting a huge chunk of steak into a vegeteraian's mouth. It got spat out pretty quickly and with much venom.

"Then, this morning, I was awoken by some silly little girl who wants to write a piece for one of these rag sheets about the so called new black militancy. She thinks it's really trendy and all she wants is an in. She'll be our friend for as long as we're in fashion then she'll be onto the next thing. I don't trust these white liberals who sniff around us and our culture, they make me sick."

I ignored the bait for I was determined not to be dragged into one, the simple fact being that the Sandra business had definitely put my mood into some shadings which were not at all conducive towards a verbal argy bargy.

Daddy Cecil was not to be put off.

"Why does whitey want to be our friend?" he asked, out loud and to noone in particular, shaking his head and examining the ingredients of his Ribena carton as if the answer was somehow to be found there.

"I know they like to bed our women because they haven't stopped that particular activity since slavery when they raped every black sister in sight. Naturally, when it's the other way round and a brother wants to check one of their women, why then boy, you'd better watch out. But everything is alright for the white boy. He's still checking our sisters, I see."

Daddy Cecil was something of a regular at the Unity Club and kept an eye on a lot of people's runnings, my business with

Sandra included, and so when I muttered, "easy," under my breath, he knew he had hit a raw nerve and pounced like a bass line right on top of the beat.

"Ah yes," he pointedly said, glancing over my way, "our sisters are much in demand these days amongst the white boys trying to make up for the sins of their forefathers."

My tongue moved without prompting as I saw red, not black, in front of me.

"Perhaps if the sisters were better treated by their so called brothers," I stated, looking straight at Daddy C., "then they wouldn't be crossing the tracks in such great numbers and leaving them behind."

In an instant Daddy C.'s face turned serious and he started in on me.

"What do you know about the sisters?" he demanded, "or the black man, come to that?"

But before I could drop a line like, "only what a 1000 sisters have told me," or something equally as stupid because, face it, guys treated gals the same the world over and nothing it is to do with colour, Brother P. was ordering us to cool it, cool it and cool it. Daddy C. kept staring hard at me as I agreed we should drop it but he knew the value of getting in the last word, after all he had studied many politicians, and he wasn't going to throw away the chance.

"Trouble with a lot of people in this town," he said, "they think everything is cool and irie but they know jack shit. You should come round my yard. Large council estate, no one works and there's a fucking war going down between us and the so called civilized white majority. We're getting cuffed up every day, families, children, the lot and no one wants to help us. Not the pigs or anyone. The day we break free from this hell is the day we will start to live and the only way to do that is to unite amongst ourselves and break free. You see, Mr. DJ Man, you don't check it, do you?"

I couldn't resist his question.

"How do you mean?"

"You play black music, seen?"

"Yeah."

"So how many black DJ's you know?"

I couldn't argue on that point because Daddy C. was stone cold correct. There were very few blacks manning the dex at clubs and it was the same, right across the board, wherever you looked. My momentary silence signalled victory for Daddy Cecil but before he could exult, Brother P. suddenly put in, "I read a report the other day which showed that there was one group of people which the cops hassle more than anyone. And that's the Irish."

Just then, and before I could add anything else, a white girl entered the cafe and came over to the table.

"Hi," she said, sitting down next to us. "Thank you for showing up for the interview. I was sure that you would not come."

Daddy C. didn't even look at her but sensing our chance to break away, Brother P. said, "Well, we'll leave you to it," and with that we rose to our feet because although Daddy C.s grievances could be heard right across the Kingdom, and, unfortunately, had much substance to them, the fact still remained that he was not a man you could sit, eat and parlare with without voices being raised or tempers being disturbed.

I went to touch skin in a gesture of friendship but he simply kissed his teeth, said, "That's right, walk away from the truth," and, with that, we walked out into the market. On the quiet journey back to Westward Ho, Brother P. had nada to say about Daddy Cecil although I was still burning at his off hand treatment and it was only when we reached Oxford St. that Brother P. announced, "You know, you can't apply Afro American politics to this tight little island. It doesn't work," and on that note we set sail for Davey Boy's, a tailor that we both use when the bank account is full, healthy and bouncy bouncy. Davey Boy is the complete East Ender, a breed unto themselves, reared on their own strict traditions and, especially in Davey's case, with a real sense of pride about the East End's involvement in fashion. As he never tired of telling us, the skinhead, suedehead and soulboy, (the tribe called S he named it) had all been born round his way and then spread, in different variations, right across the country.

Although they had lost the casual to South London, no doubt somewhere in the East End, someone was planning a new look and style for, after all, at the heart of the area is a thriving rag trade and a black market, all of which need constant nourishment.

Davey Boy, himself, was a motor mouth with balls who, as far as we were concerned, came from the right side of the tracks for it wasn't that long ago he had been arrested for fighting fascist skinheads.

"Not right, is it?" he once explained to us, "going round calling people all kinds of names and beating the shit out of them because of the skin they were given. Fucking ridiculous. That kind of thing really offends me. Now, my grandfather, God rest his soul, that's a different kettle of poisson altogether.

"Dear old boy but he was a nutter and he loved to rumble. Joined up as one of Oswald's boys, didn't he, until he was made to see sense but, as I always say, we all take a wrong turning in life and as long as you realise you've gone astray and try and do something about it, then it's not the end of the world by a long mark."

To give the man his laurels, Davey knew his gears inside out. All you had to give him was a year, say 1963, and he could tell you, on the spot, exactly what fashions were going off, who was running the scene and where it all went. Better still, just mention a film or a well known personage from the distant past, and he knew the design inside and out.

"Jacket like Sammy Davis's in A Man Called Adam, no problemo."

Davey Boy was an invaluable time box to the last thirty years, a man who could lead you like a child through a staggering array of styles and fashions and, what's more, knew exactly what you were after just by the reference points you dropped.

What's more, he was a hustler supremo whose every action was dictated by the colour of money and so, even though I didn't trust him as far as I could throw him, the charm and cheek made him impossible to dislike.

On this particular occasion, as we strolled in, Davey Boy welcomed us both with numerous pins jutting out of his mouth In front of him stood a tall, blond haired, blue eyes specimen who stood as straight as Nelson's column as Davey Boy pinned cloth against him.

Davey Boy motioned hello to us, unable to parlare until his work was finished and, on which occasion, he then greeted us with a boisterous, "Hello there, chaps," a definite touch of the upper class accent very discernible in his voice.

Brother P. and I cottoned on straight away as to the social standing of his customer as Davey continued his line.

"Now then, sir, on the sleeve, how many buttons would sir like? One? Two? Or maybe we might want to think about going out on the limb somewhat and adding four buttons. What does sir think?"

"Just the one will be fine," came the booming reply, the depth and command of the voice betraying army roots. In his hand he held a cloth version of the family crest which the toff had decided should be displayed on the jacket's top pocket as pater and mater would undoubtedly be absolutely thrilled to see it shown off in public.

Trying to figure out why this upper class specimen from the

realms of high society was not down at Hacketts with the rest of the braying bunch, Brother P. and I began examining the long rolls of cloth that Davey had stacked against the walls whilst a mix of envy and hatred began to surface in my stomach.

I know it's uncool and everything to judge a man's soul by his accent but from where I've been standing these past few years, whichever way you checked it, these people, the rich and privileged had been handed the sweetie jar the day they were born and they were not about to share out the goodies.

What's more, it was their set up, from the playing fields of Eton to the company boardroom, that kept out anyone with infinite more imagination and intelligence from getting to where they wanted. No doubt about it, the higher you climbed in this society the stupider the people became, and that's the truth, Ruth.

Not only were they mostly a bunch of hypocrites, prattling on about morals and the like whilst they are robbing some company account blind and knocking off the gardener or the maid, but the codes of conduct and routine they had devised were like antiquated children's games.

Next time you're there check out the House Of Lords or Parliament and all that eyes to the right, eyes to the left, don't walk in front of him and remember to bow routine that goes on, all put there so that they can go from public school to parliament, and never know the difference. If truth be known, such people, removed as they are from life's edges, ups and downs, circles and squares, I sometimes feel a little sorry for because, face it, you've got to be half a robot to go through with it all in the first place, although please don't get me wrong, I'd rather go forty days and nights without hearing a decent tune than ever feel total simpatico with the likes of Lord Haw Haw that Davey Boy was now attending to.

It was time, I decided, for some class warfare.

"Oi, Davey Boy," I called across the shop in my best Cockney accent, "comin' dawn the pub for a shandy later?"

The man of cloth, spotting the game that was afoot, quickly put me out of play by shooting me a glance of such withering contempt that in an instant, I felt like a kid caught pissing in the sink, and so I ended further communicado until Lord Haw Haw was up and finished and striding out of the shop.

"Don't wind up the punters," complained Davey Boy, wrapping away the cloth, "you'll only put me out of pocket plus it ruins all my chances of breaking into the deb's circuit and finding myself a little wild child who can keep me in a style that I am unaccustomed to, know what I mean?"

It was true that Davey Boy was on the lookout for a partner for he had recently left his wife of nine months standing, his explanation for this whirlwind marriage being based on the fact that he and his sweetheart had been longtime lovers but once the knot had been tied, the magic suddenly vanished and they drifted apart.

The other story doing the rounds told a different tale. This story had Davey Boy come home one night to find his beloved, drunk in bed, wearing a newly bought leather biker's jacket. Davey Boy, who is allergic to all motorbike or rocker gear, demanded that either the jacket went or he did.

As no coat has yet been designed to stand up and transport itself when asked, and as the wife had just raided the holiday cashola to buy it, Davey Boy had no choice but to accept his wife's stern refusal and leave the field of play, hence his current enthusiasm to resume action on the gal front and find someone caked up enough to help him out on the alimony deal now heading his way.

"Anyway, I'm glad you've strolled in because I want a word in both your shellikes, if you don't mind."

"Sure, Davey Boy," I replied, "but only if you tell us what Lord Haw Haw was doing here. I mean it's hardly his neck of the woods."

"Well, that's what I wanted to talk to you about. Have you heard about this Acid House scene that's starting up? I need to know if it's a goer or not."

"That must be the club Dillon was about," I said to Brother P.

"Why are you interested?" asked my companion.

"See, the other night I went out with my kid brother. I see a lot more of the kid now that I'm at home and he hates it because I'm always taking the piss out of him in front of his little girlfriends. I say little but you should see some of them. You'd get arrested if you didn't know their age.

"Anyway, one night I'm bored and that, so I tag along with him to this club round our way. I used to go there myself so that shows you how far I've come in life. Still, they say everything goes round in circles.

"Now, I'm not kidding you but it was un-be-fucking-lieviable down there. There's all these young'uns, togged up like farmers in baggy jeans and dungarees, off their heads and going absolutely mad. They were all over the shop. You could tell. Their eyes were shot and they didn't have a care in the world. Friendly as fuck, mind you, no bother whatsoever.

"Anyways, the place is rammed and there's dry ice everywhere and these bleedin' strobe lights going off every five seconds. You remember them don't you? Nah, course you don't, you were just a twinkle in your dad's bollocks then but you know the sort I mean. Ones that flash all the time and you get a fucking great headache watching them.

"Anyways, it was manic down there so I pulled my kid brother aside and asked him, what the fuck is going on? You know what he does? He pulls out these three white pills and tells me that at least three quarters of the bods there have dropped one and that's why everyone is going beserk. They're called Ecstasy and aparently you don't give a fuck once you've dropped it or as my kid brother says, got right on one.

"Doesn't sound right to me. I mean, in my day, it was blues that did the trick but this stuff is something else. I dunno, maybe I'm getting on but I told him if I saw him dropping one I'd make his life hell rather than ecstasy."

"So what had this got to do with Lord Haw Haw?" I enquired. Davey Boy put down the cloth and gave a knowing smile.

"I've got a mate, see, who hires out equipment for weddings and knees up. Anyway, the other day he got a call from some toff who was in a right two and eight because all the gear he'd ordered for some end of term ball hadn't turned up.

"So my mate bells me and off we go down to Putney to this really posh college with huge lawns and a river. All the geezers are in penguin suits, the birds have got the gowns on and by the time we've set everything up, everyone is on the champers and it's roaring.

"Me and my mate have got nothing to do now except make sure that nothing breaks down so we have a few shandies and the next thing I know I'm half pissed and telling Lord Haw Haw that that I could make him a jacket that would piss over any Saville Row job. I give him my card and then I don't see him again.

"I woke up the next day feeling like shit and I'm sitting in here drinking coffee, trying to recover when who should walk in but Lord Haw Haw there. Turns out he was one of the organisers of the do and they had run into a spot of bother because some little oik had strolled in there and took a load of happy snaps of them all completely off their nuts and groping each other. I was so pissed I didn't see any of this going on but the happy snapper has only sold the photos to one of the dailies.

"If the photos had been in the local rag you wouldn't particularly give a fuck, would you? But if your mummy and daddies are the ones who are caked up to the eyeballs and running the show over at Westminster, it's a different story, innit?

"Anyway, old Lord Haw Haw has had a few irate pater and maters on the phone and the college head is right on his case. So now he's figuring the best thing to do is get out while the going's good and find something else to get into. I mean the guy maybe slow on the uptake but he knows one thing, money makes money. So while I'm decking him out, he starts picking my brains for some new angle.

"That night I go out with my kid brother to that club and I'm sitting there amongst all this madness thinking of some way of getting in with the geezer and, suddenly, it hits me. There it is right, in front of me. Get in on this Acid House thing now. So what I need to know is whether you think this scene is going to last. I mean, look at punk. If you had got in there right at the start there's no knowing where you'd be now."

Throughout this speed spiel Brother P. and I exchanged bewildering glances as we were not too sure where Davey Boy was going but as his verbal jigsaw came together we had to tell truth that we were not particularly sure about this latest development on the teen scene but if we had any thoughts on the matter then Davey Boy would be the first to know.

"By the way," I said, "have you had any luck with that original Dormeuil tonic material I was after?"

"Can't say I have as yet," Davey Boy replied, "but I've heard about a little warehouse I'm going to have a snoop around soon, so give me a shout next week. see if we can't come up with something. Here, how's the club doing? I might pass by soon and shake a leg, you never know. Mind you, the reports I've heard about your DJ'ing you'd be better off mixing in the kitchen than on a turntable. See ya next week, boys."

Making our exit with Davey Boy slapping us on our shoulders, Brother P. and I ventured onto Oxford St., discussing Davey Boy's proposal and trying to figure out whether he was onto something, which, to tell truth, we couldn't really see.

"Workways is bestways for me," Brother P. then announced, "I've got a few loose things to tie up," and, agreeing to parlare with each other before the day's sun was down and out, we parted company.

"Hey," shouted the man as I walked off, "take it easy now. Things will be cool."

I couldn't share his optimism but I didn't want him to check that so I signalled back my agreement with a raised hand and made tracks to Tottenham Court Tube leaving him to hustle up work and the old cashola.

I should add here that the Brother P. could not and would not let himself be defined by the nature of his job as most numbers are, if only because his work was so varied that no single title had yet been invented to encompass all his known activities.

The only connecting factor to all his various dealings was, I suppose, the music game. One week would find him running on errands for some record company, placing a tune of theirs with all the right people, whilst the next he would be handing out flyers for a one off club he would be setting up, always observing his golden rule by dropping off free tickets at the model agencies.

"A club full of women is the only club both men and women want to go to," the Brother P, explained and, indeed, on the nights I had helped out as a warm up DJ I had seen his theory work beautifully in practise. People were always bugging about when the next event would be but Brother P. knew the value of not overloading and so his sporadic events were always something special.

He was as obssessed with music as I was and through this mutual love we had developed, over the years, our own little code. For the example, certain frames of mind were defined by the overall tone of a particular artist's work.

If you were feeling Stevie (Wonder) then you were happy with the world and your place in it. If a Marvin (Gaye) was approaching then it was odds on that you were moving into a reflective spiritual state usually brought about by a gal, whilst a Nina (Simone) denoted a bad one, a time of darkness that only her pain filled voice could crack open and bring in the light. You certainly needed a Curtis (Mayfield) to help you recuperate or maybe a touch of Sly (Stone) would do the trick.

Such was the tone of our friendship whose roots stretched back to the same part of London that we inhabited although we were never as linked up in those times as we are now.

This was back in the days, when we were both based around Kentish Town and well before my P&M decided to cash in their chips and travel around the world as a lifetime reward for hard work (dad was a printer, mum, a nurse) and raising myself in times both happy and harsh.

Going about our separate runnings, many was the time that Brother P. and I would pass each other on the street, slyly checking out each other's gears but never letting a word pass between us, such is our nature.

It was, of all people, a group of striking miners that brought us together and God bless them for doing so as well as giving Mrs. T. a real run for her money.

Now, in the matter of politics, I have to relate that I was raised on a steady and balanced diet of Socialism and although I am not au fait with all the ins and outs, the names and dates, I must state that when my father, a union rep, no less, parlared with me on the subject, I automatically thought it natural, as I do to this day, that some kind of equality amongst the people was a given neccessary if you wanted a society to function in a cool and collected manner.

Furthermore, when you checked it, some of the top guys and gals to have walked amongst us, Jesus, Gandhi, Martin Luther King, Malcolm X., and all the other brave souls who put their lives on the line, were basically of the same opinion, and I am certainly not about to argue with them on the subject.

I realise of course that in this day and age such views are held to be old fashioned, but there are some fundamentals, (and I can hear my father talking now) that you have to defend and live by.

For my parents, Margaret Thatcher was the last straw. "Look at her eyes," my father would exclaim when she came on TV, "they're not only evil but they're unbalanced. Mark my words. She'll ransack this country and then walk away leaving us all in the shit."

This, coupled with the feeling that he and mum could never shake off, namely that this country treated everyone like a child who had to be in bed by ten at the latest, forced their hand, and they fled to more civilised climates, places where you can get a coffee at two in the morning or walk the street late at night without being hassled by the cops.

I fully agreed with my parent's decision to split but I have to say that everytime I pass Big Ben, I have to resist the urge to pop in and harangue the collected MPs for letting people as good as my parents just up and leave, for this country is so much poorer without the likes of them, and I won't hear any different.

It took me a long time to suss out that every political team was simply there to maintain the staus quo although I must just add that I would never waste my vote given the people down the ages who have fought for us to have that right. The least we can do is mark a piece of paper every four years, if only in memory of their indomitable spirit, although Brother P. had come to these conclusions a lot earlier than me and had decided to live, as most do now, by his own rules and regulations, come hell or high water.

Which is why, in 1985, we linked up by Kentish Town tube station. The miners' strike was about halfway through and in an effort to keep them going, some miners had travelled south and set up stalls all over town to raise money, food and clothing for the fight.

On a bitterly cold day I had arisen at an early hour to go and lend some of my time to their cause and, on reaching their stall, found that the Brother P. had beaten me by a good five minutes and was busy handing over a bag full of sandwiches, cakes, fruit and plantain.

"That's really good of you," the young, fresh faced miner who was manning the stall, was telling him, "it's not often you see your kind..."

"Our kind," said the Brother P. automatically, "our kind."

The miner looked at the man in front of him and recognised a new breed of Briton, different colour but British all the same. He extended his hand. "You're right my friend, our kind it is."

These were the early days of the strike, a testing lull before battle proper commenced and this country's working class showed, once again, the way forward. The war might have been lost but in battle their sense of unity was a real and true testament to how easily people can come together and if that sounds naive, then so be it. Never let anyone tell you different, for that, such as making the poor feel guilty about having money, is just another ploy by the rich to keep their loot.

At the stall, I had no choice but to break the ice between us and say, "Alright, nice pair of strides you got on."

The man didn't even glance down at his blue and grey Prince of Wales check number, but simply replied, "Yeah?" in that familiar questioning tone I have come to know so well. We left it at that.

Over the next few weeks we nodded to each other when we passed until it became crystal clear that the silence would have to be broken, which it was in a record shop where we bumped into each other whilst simultaneously reaching for a copy of The Isley Brothers album, "Black Berries".

Brother P. said, "Cool, you take it. I know where I can get another copy."

"Where's that?" I enquired and we were off and running, parlaring about this, that and the other. We ended up back at my home as my P&M were both at work. I skinned up a huge joint in celebration of our link, smoked off a bit and then offered it to him.

"No thanks, I don't. It fuddles the brain too much."

He left me ten minutes later staring up at the ceiling.

I had just started DJ'ing and my financial position was such that I was required to stay at home. This was cool with my folks but as they were itching to go AWOL and put their feet up on some large cruiser and watch the world go by, I was looking to move.

It was the Brother P. who threw me a lifeline by securing me a spot at The Unity and pointing me towards my flat on the Stroud Green, P&M helping out with the deposit and a month's rent, which is where I was now heading for.

It was now 2.30 p.m. and as I hit the Stroud Green concrete, brilliant sunshine poured down onto the street, cutting through the fading crisp air. It was delightfully warm but very unsettling because February had no business being this hot and everyone around you knew it.

It was the most serious sign that seasonal changes, the secure routine of winter, spring, summer and autumn, which as a child you set your watch and life to, was now under threat and when something as fundamental as the world's temperature starts to malfunction, a quiet panic slowly envelopes you. When you consider that the problemo is man made you get even more panicky. Everyone knows about man's capacity to destroy, but, sad to say, the judges are still out on his ability to see the light and start the healing.

A shrinking, bleeding ozone layer shrank the future and was yet another 20th century concern that made you want to holler at the way they did your life.It detonated inside you the kind of shock feelings you get when someone you know unexpectedly dies and in a terrible flash you clearly felt and saw how fragile life truly is, and what's the point of making plans or dreaming dreams if that's how it is, which, let's face it, is not the most healthy way to conduct your affairs.

That said there was a real rush to be had by the scenery that swarmed around me as Africans strolled the streets in their traditional gears, and then there was the local guys and gals all dressed up as if they had just stepped off the set of the latest Spike Lee flick, old looking Greek guys disappearing into shops where the windows were all blacked out, shopkeepers shooting the breeze with their customers, children chasing each other in and out of the other shoppers who cursed them out, and not to forget the old folk who, like the young, had their own particular dress code.

It was like being in a film with so many characters to grab your attention that my mind was totally elsewhere when my heart dropped a beat and I realised that the very serious gal standing outside my front door was none other than Sandra.

"Hi," she said, as I caught up with her. I said nothing, simply nodded at her and opened up the door, leaving it open for her to follow me up.

This she did, locating herself in my front room whilst I made for the bedroom where I keep basic coffee making equipment, utensils, I ruefully noted, that I had used not so long ago as she lay sleeping in my bed.

As I made the coffee I had the notion to try and keep everything formal between us as if we were two people who had just met and were about to have a coffee before we got down to business. I still have no idea where these crazy ideas come from.

"What have you been up to?" I asked her as I came in with the coffee. Sandra sat on my small sofa amidst the mess of records, sleeves, magazines, cassettes and opened envelopes.

"Nothing much," she replied, taking her coffee. "Just getting on with things. How about you?"

She nodded to the three record boxes over by the dex.

"Still DJ'ing I see."

"Yeah, normal runnings. Been going out at all?"

"Nah, I've had other things on my mind."

We sat in silence, the tension between us as palpable as the hot cups we held for we both had seperate programmes to follow and were determined to do so, whatever the cost. It was time to get into one.

"So what are you going to do about this mess we're in?"

"Jesus," she angrily shot back, "do you have to be so off all the time? I am pregnant, you know."

"Yeah, I heard. Someone told me. Congratulations. I hope you'll both be very happy."

"Don't be sarcastic, it doesn't become you."

"Well, as far as I remember you were taking certain precautions. That's what you said, yes? Or perhaps I heard you wrong."

Sandra leapt off the sofa.

"You calling me a fucking liar? Eh? Is that it? Think I'm trying to trap you do you? Don't flatter yourself, sugar. I'm only dealing with you because of an accident. OK? It was an accident. Shit. You think I want a baby by you? Cha! I'd find better men than you living off the street."

"Well, why don't you fuck off and find them?"

"Don't you dare use language like that in front of me. Or my baby."

"Oh, so it's your baby now, is it?"

"Well you don't want it, do you? You got what you wanted and now look at you running a mile. Men! You make me sick, the lot of you."

By now, we were standing up, facing each other in a red hot

war of the words and it was getting us absolutely nowhere.

"Shit," I said, sitting down for we both needed to cool it and try another way. Sandra must have thought so as well because she resumed her position on the sofa.

"Have you got any cigarettes?" she asked.

I reached into my bag and we lit up.

"What does your mum think. Have you told her yet?"

"This morning. She's actually quite pleased. She'll stand by me."

"Have you thought at all about not having the baby," I asked in a quiet voice, sensing that the time was right.

Sandra sighed.

"Of course I've considered it. I've thought about a lot of things ever since I found out. That's why I came to see you. See if we can't find a way through."

"What do you think? Is that a possibility?"

"I really don't know if I can do it. Just after my dad fucked off, my sister got pregnant and had to have one. She said it was the most painful thing she'd ever been through mentally as well as physically. It's human life we're talking about here."

"I haven't got any money, you know."

Sandra kissed her teeth in disgust, her expression changing to one of pure frustration, like a teacher talking to a child who simply refuses to listen and has now used up all the tricks of the trade to get through.

What depressed me about it all was that throughout the whole bitter exchange, I had discreetly, against my wishes I must add, been checking out Sandra's form, just as I had on the fateful night we met, and although my gaze kept returning to her shapely legs and pretty little face, I have to say that I felt nothing.

It made me sad that I could not tap into my first feelings towards her for that would have at least helped me understand better the wild dilemma I found myself in.

It was not to be. All I wanted at this precise moment in time was Sandra out of the flat and out of my life but that kind of scene is for the movies and the movies only.

"I have to be somewhere soon," I said nonchalantly.

Sandra looked at me for a good five seconds, stood up, crossed the room to where I was sitting and said, "I came here to try and reason with you but as you seem incapable of doing that, perhaps this will make you understand that you can not treat people like throwaway rubbish."

Then she pulled back her hand and gave me the hardest slap on the face that I have ever recieved. Then she walked, slamming all doors on her way out.

A red hot fire spread across my face and a buzzing sound started up in my mind, getting louder and louder and louder until I could stand it no more. I jumped up, pulled down my window and shouted, in the direction I presumed she was heading, "Don't you ever come back here you stupid fucking bitch or I'll kill you, I swear it."

I yanked down the window and made for the phone book. Picking out her number I dialled it and got, as I hoped I would, her machine.

"You bitch, don't ever let me see you again or you'll regret it. Badly."

I slammed down the phone and spent the next few minutes stalking my small front room, kicking objects out of the way and punching walls until the rage finally subsided.

I know, I know, uncool behaviour most certainly but when you reach that pitch where you find yourself consumed with so much anger that you're dangerously out of control, then it's best to let it all out then and there. If you don't it will only come out later and some innocent victim is going to cop it for no reason at all.

Only it wasn't just anger coursing through my veins but a real confusion as well, tangled up with feelings of guilt and recrimination, until, unable to stand it any further, I grabbed my spliff tin, built a peace pipe that Sitting Bull would have been proud of and, taking time to place some suitable musica on the dex, I lay on my sofa waiting for the magical smoke to take me somewhere better.

At first, the smoke brought on feelings of fear for the future but that soon evaporated as it swarmed around my brain and I closed my eyes and drifted off into darkness.

When I came to, which was about three hours later, dusk was creeping through my window, darkening my room and everything in it. The Stroud Green Road traffic was now reduced to a passing car every minute or so and the street lights were on.

All of which meant that it was time to wander down to Bee Wee's, pick up some rotis, chicken and rice and then, in the fading London gloom, stroll casually back to my yard and listen to some tunes before heading out.

In the middle of this relaxed schedule I belled the Brother P. and he duly arrived at about 10.00, just as Westwood was signing off his radio show. After a quick spliff for me and a shot of rum for him, we headed out in his wheels to the club Dillon had told us about.

On the way down he asked me about the rest of the day's events and I related to him my unhappy fable. After it had come to its unresolved finish, Brother P. nodded and said, "I spoke to that chick who knows Sandra and she swears that she is not one for moving around a lot. As far as she could check it, Sandra is a one man woman."

"Well, she was pretty live and direct with me."

"All I can say to that, my brother, is that she must have liked you an awful lot."

I shrugged my shoulders, announced to my erstwhile companion that I didn't want to think about it anymore and settled back to watch London flash past my window, once again finding myself amazed at how we always miss what is right under our very chins, for there are times when I clock certain parts of this old, majestic and mystic town which make me believe I must be in a dream, so rare are the sights.

As in right now as we turned into Trafalgar Square and caught sight of the National Portrait gallery, its white towering presence beautifully illuminated by powerful hidden lights, giving off the notion that the brickwork had somehow soaked in all the events and secrets of the last thousand years and was now slowly breathing them out again.

Brother P. caught my mood.

"City's nice tonight," he muttered as if he was the only person alive on earth and we journeyed Southside in silence, wrapped up in blankets of our own thoughts.

When the mood takes us we can both be very short on words but that is not a problemo for us as we both understand the value of silence which sometimes is just as valuable as speech.

Parking up the four wheeler, we strolled down to the club, a converted gym situated down a small alley. A familiar scene, that of people crowding around the entrance trying to make their way past two unsmiling, untalkative bouncers, greeted us and it made me glad to be with the Brother P. for he is on first name terms with everyone on the club circuit and this included the bouncer Chris, who, with a slight nod of the head, made space for us to step through and down some steps to the cloakroom.

The girl taking the coats was so vague as to where the cloakroom tickets were that in the end Brother P. kissed his teeth in disgust and we walked through some double doors into the club, carrying our coats.

"She's off her head," Brother P. said as I surveyed the club whose layout was totally different from The Unity's. Directly in front of us was a bar area whilst to the right a longish, thin corridor took you down to the dancefloor area.

To be God's honest such details were nothing compared to the noise and energy which assaulted you the minute you walked in. Over by the bar, young herberts, stripped down to just t shirts and jeans, their jumpers loosely tied around their waist, gulped at small bottles of lucozade or water, laughing raucously and often, slapping each other on the back and hugging each other as if they had just scored the winning goal at Wembley.

Over by the tables, people sat excitedly round in groups, shouting to each other as if their lives depended on getting their point of view over, whilst other couples embraced kissing each other up as if they were in the sanctuary of their own private boudoir.

To reach the dancefloor you had to push your way down that crowded corridor and what really took your attention was that the guys who stood pinned against the wall, many of them topless and with tatoos to display, were precisely the kind of geezers you crossed the road to avoid if you saw them coming towards you in packs of more than one.

Not this time. As we moved slowly down that packed corridor, far from getting the hump because you happened to look at the colour of their shoes, they started making way, shouting, "You alright, mate?" and "How's it going? It's fucking great here, innit?"

The dancefloor was something else. Filled with dry ice which you could hear sho-ssing out of somewhere or other, the large speakers pumped House music's primal beat to a crowd that couldn't stop filling the air with wild whoops of delight. Above them, strobe lights flickered on and off every five minutes or so, the light distorting their crazy movements into slow motion.

But that was nothing to the eruption that occured when the DJ, a face I had never seen before, kicked off a tune that began with a loud but distant voice, (one of The Jacksons, no less) shouting, "Can you feel it?" and the crowd literally went wild, as the tune's hard but staggered beats came roaring in and the crowd danced like their lives depended on it.

It was the total opposite of the cool manner that pervades most London clubs and it was dangerously fascinating to watch. It was as if the people had become children again, unfettered by manners or hangups and not concerned with what anybody thought of them. They were there to party forever and it gave the club a sense of wildness that I had never witnessed before.

It was not to the Brother P.'s taste. "Man, I'm outta here," he shouted in my ear. "This is craziness."

"Stay a bit," I remonstrated for I was hypnotised by the energy in front of me and I wanted to check it further, but once the Brother P. has his mind set neither Muhammad or the mountain can move him.

"Nah," he answered, "I'm chipping. Check you, tomorrow."

"Laters."

I positioned myself in the corner just as the cloakroom girl appeared out of the mist and pointed her finger to a point high above my head, saying, "Isn't it beautiful, so very beautiful."

I glanced up and saw that she was talking about the strobe light. "Yes," I replied, not really believing the conversation, and I moved off towards the bar as the lights were now seriously doing my head in.

As I made my way down the corridor of herberts, the noise of their words ricocheting off the walls at an incredible volume, I spotted Dillon coming into the club and disappearing into the bar.

I made my way through and tapped him on the shoulder.

"How's it going?"

"Good man, good.I didn't think you'd come here. What do you think?"

"Of the club? It's mad. I've never seen a crowd like this or heard any of the music. I can't get to grips with this one."

"Take one of these and you will."

Dillon reached into his pocket and carefully pulled out two white pills. "I got them this evening. Twenty quid each."

"Jesus, that's a lot of cashola."

"Fucking worth it. I was going to take two but you have one."

Now on the drugs tip I operate by a no chemical policy, sticking to a mix of herb and rum which always does the trick as far as I'm concerned and, what's more, doesn't, like some drugs, leave you staring at a wall which then turns into a mass of writhing snakes which proceed to wrap themselves around your neck.

A 16 year old kid at school convinced me of this policy. One bright day, he dropped an acid tab and then jumped off the top of a six storey car park convinced he could fly.

They buried him a week later.

Therefore, I find myself at this juncture, completely unable to tell you why I picked up one of the tablets, examined it, handed a score over to Dillon, and then popped it into my mouth as if I was taking a headache pill.

Maybe it was the day's events that had pushed me and it was my subconscious trying to forget the last twelve hours. Or, perhaps, there are some things in life that simply have no rhyme or reason and that when you really check it, that's what makes it such a kick because you never really know what is going to happen from one day to the next. It is only when you stop and look back at the tapestry of your life that you start to see how random so many events are, and even though each and every one of us map out in our heads the road we want to follow, we are always being sidetracked by obstacles we know nothing of.

That's when you start to get an inkling of the invisible forces that can, if the mood takes them, move us around like chess pieces, blowing us here, there and everywhere, and all of us powerless to resist.

"What happens now?"

"Nothing," Dillon replied.

"Nothing?"

"For now, nothing. Half an hour and then it'll kick off, the best fucking feeling in the world."

"Right. Let's get a drink then."

"Look," Dillon carefully said, "the worst thing you can do is worry. Just relax. It'll be fine. Everybody else is on it and they seem to be doing alright to me."

He turned and I followed him to the bar not failing to notice against the corridor wall a couple viciously kissing each other up, seemingly unperturbed that everyone could easily spot the guy's hand slipping purposefully up his gal's skirt.

"How does this shit work?" I asked Dillon as I joined him at the bar for now, truth be told, I was dreading what I had let myself in for.

"Well, stay off the alcohol or orange juice because that works against it. Pretty soon you'll get a rush and you'll feel yourself about to go. You'll also want a shit like nobody's business but that disappears in a minute. After that, you're up and away. But the worst thing you can do is worry. Go with it, man, go with it."

"Have you done it a lot?"

"Four times. This is my fifth. Believe me man it's wicked. I dropped one last night."

"Yeah, we noticed."

"When?"

"This morning, in the shop."

"You came in?"

You could see Dillon searching his brain for confirmation of my statement and it was not a pretty sight. I panicked even further.

"Look Dillon, how can I get rid of this?"

"You can't. But stop the worry. Look around you. No-one's dead are they? No-one's being carted off to hospital. You're too cool for your own good. Relax. Everything is fine. It's a wicked feeling. Everyone here will tell you the same thing."

"I know," I replied, gazing over at a group of herberts, one of whom was now indulging in a mock striptease to the loud encouragement of all his friends.

"It's like this lot have just discovered there's more to life than bloodshed down The Shed at Chelsea on a Saturday afternoon."

"They've been coming here since the club started. You wouldn't believe it, would you? Ecstasy has done more to put them on the right track than anything or anybody ever will."

"Jesus," I put in, "you sound like Timothy Leary."

"Whose he? A DJ?" Taking our soft drinks, we found a vacant table and started parlaring on the usual subject of our respective business, Dillon filling me in on some up and coming releases, how the shop was doing, and more chit-chat, chit-chat, chit-chat, when suddenly, about twenty minutes into the conversation my stomach suddenly turned warm, as if someone had just lit a small fire inside, and I began taking deep breaths hoping that the the smoke filled air would somehow extinguish the sensation.

Dillon noted me with a knowing smile, reaching inside his pocket and pulling out a pack of gum at precisely the moment my teeth started to grind. Hastily, I stuffed a stick into my mouth and began chewing hard. The next thing I knew a huge yawn, like I had not slept for fifteen days, opened up my mouth and, as I started to stretch, another yawn hit me, and then another and another and another, until I felt a violent urge to visit the gents, which I somehow resisted before it mercifully passed away.

Like an electric shock, the pill had disconnected me to everything around me and all I could do was stare at my glass until, with a hard jolt, I became acutely aware of the sheer cacophony of noise around me, as if I was able to pick up on any conversation, in any part of the bar, and tune into it.

I gazed around me at all the guys and gals present and

somehow they didn't seem real at all. I could hear them but they appeared distant and dreamlike. Another urge hit me and this time it was to run my fingers through my hair, which I did for a minute, marvelling at the sensation whilst chewing even harder on my gum.

I looked up to see Dillon smiling at me and realised that all the time this was happening, I had completely forgotten he was there.

"What's up?" I asked him. "I asked you two minutes ago if you wanted a drink and all you did was stare at the glass and then push your hair back. You've started early, it hasn't hit me yet. Also your eyes have gone a bit weird."

"Get us a lemonade," I urged him,

"Alright, alright," he said, patting me on the arm.

"I'll pay, I'll pay. I don't mind but I don't think I can move."

"That's cool, I'll get them."

"You sure, yeah? It's just that..."

"I know," said Dillon smiling as he went off in search of refreshment.

As I sat there, from out of nowhere I felt a huge wave sweep up inside my body and literally knock me backwards against the wall.

I was gulping for breath when Dillon returned with the drinks. "I'm getting the rushes," he said, sitting down. "Jesus, they're strong."

The both of us sat there in complete silence for about five minutes, staring into space, completely removed from all that was going on around us. I had never felt anything like it before.

All of a sudden, without any warning, this dreamlike state stopped and it was as if I suddenly clicked into life.

I had been AWOL from the world, and no doubt about it, but a new sensation was now starting to come through and I could feel myself being taken over by an indescribable energy, a force so positive that I had to release it there and then.

"Come on," I said to Dillon, who looked like he was just coming to after a three rounder with the world champ, "I want to go and see what's happening."

He looked up at me.

"Too fucking right," and with that we exited the bar and started to push down the still heaving corridor, only this time I wore a huge grin because now I could understand everything I had witnessed earlier and, stranger still, felt a camaraderie for every smiling herbert I passed. As I jostled through the crowd I heard a noise behind me and turned to see that Dillon's feet had been taken from beneath him by some carelessly spilt drink. In a flash, four people were helping him to his feet, asking if he was hurt, did he need to sit down for a bit, would he be alright and all the time, Dillon was laughing hysterically. I too saw the funny side and felt a surge of real companionship towards the guy, and, what's more, couldn't help but express it when we finally reached the dancefloor.

"You know Dillon," I shouted earnestly to him, "ever since I've been going into your shop I've always checked for you. You never try and rip us off, man and I appreciate that."

"Thanks man," he replied, putting his arm around me.

"I always like it when you come in as well. And your friend," he added, "although the both of you are far too cool sometimes. You know that, don't you?"

"Are we?"

"Yeah, sometimes you hardly say a word the pair of you. Always reserved, aren't you? But that's alright. You're both good guys."

It's funny how you can walk around in this world and believe you are one thing while all the time other people check for you in a completely different manner. One day, I mused to myself, I'd love to find people who knew me at all different ages and and sizes and see what their assessment of me was, it would tell you so much about yourself. In fact, mention of Brother P. made me wish that right at that moment he was by my side so I could relay to him my feelings towards him, how much I dug our friendship and all that good stuff, and suddenly I had a burning desire to get to a phone and bell him with the news when a tune came thundering through the speakers, and the next thing I was on the floor, dancing in abandon on a surge of energy and great self confidence.

Why, I thought to myself, I could take Sammy The Foot on here for I felt a joy for life pervade my every bone and fibre, and all around me people were obviously feeling the same because every time you looked over at someone, you would both grin and smile at each other, as if you had been friends for years.

The music started to become more urgent and I found myself locking into its relentless beat as sounds appeared from out of nowhere, like this voice demanding you to, "Move your body, move your body," and that's exactly what you did, not even caring about the sweat that you could feel trickling down your face and into the corners of your mouth. The dancing and the music took me higher and higher and as both Dillon and I began to lose ourselves, I suddenly noticed a half naked, youngish looking guy, lanky and thin with a shock of red hair, approach the large bass bin speakers and actually attempt to climb into one, his head bent low with his left ear crushed against the speaker as he literally tried to get inside the music. I went over and put my hand on his shoulder to restrain him and he looked up at me with a look of pure contentment on his face before moving off, which was when Dillon tapped me on the shoulder and motioned that he needed a drink. The sweat now pouring off my face, I realised, was major but I had no care for at this precise moment in my life I had never felt happier with myself or the world. It was as if we were in heaven.

Suddenly, Sandra was a distant problemo not even worth

thinking about so tiny was its concern to me. My belief in myself as a DJ was unshakeable and the only thought that bugged me out was, why can't life be like this all the time? What stopped us from feeling this brilliant about ourselves and others every waking minute of our lives? It was a question that I wanted to ask everyone as we happily pushed pushed our way back down the corridor and into the bar where I told Dillon to grab some seats and I'd get the juices in. One of the bar staff, a middle aged woman, came to serve me and I ordered two lemonades.

"God almighty," she cried, "what is it with you lot? Don't none of you drink or something? All I've done all night is hand out bleedin' lemonades and lucozades." "Lucozade," I said on the spur of the moment, "make it two lucozades."

"Alright dear, don't have a heart attack. Do you want some jelly to go with it?"

She went off for the drink and I fished for some coins in my pocket.

"That's two quid," she said on her quick return, putting the bottles down in front of me. I handed over the cashola and was about to move on when I heard her shout, "Oi! I said two pounds not two pence, and, sure enough, that was the exact amount I had placed in her hand.

"Oh, I'm so sorry," I said and pulled out all my change with the express and honourable intention of paying her correctly. Yet, to my great bemusement, I found myself with another problemo; I couldn't, for the life of me, distinguish one coin from the other. Everything in my hand was just a blur. As I stared down at the coinage, furiously debating what to do next, a hand appeared, picked out two, one pound coins and handed them over to the bar woman.

I turned to face a gal, young looking, short, curly blond hair, wearing dungarees and a smiley t shirt.

"They get kind of mixed up, don't they?"

"Tell me about it," I said. And then, "Who may I ask are you?"

She smiled ever so sweetly and it lit up her face. "I'm Aretha."

"Franklin!"

We both shouted it at the same time but she did so with a predictable, haven't heard that one before tone.

"Sorry," I said, "you must get that all the time."

"Tell me about it," she said trying to mimick my accent.

"Well, seeing as how you have just rescued me I think it only fair that you join myself and my good companion sitting over there for a drink. I promise that there will be no more obvious jokes."

"Promise," she said playfully, looking up at me and I couldn't but help notice her form which, covered up as it was, truly demanded another form of promise.

I felt the familiar sensation of John Thomas pass through me, heightened like never before, and suddenly all I could concentrate on was this gal. Nothing else seemed to matter. I had to get with her. I took her gently by the arm and led her over to Dillon who sat vacantly staring at the table, as if he had made a trip to Mars and was still not earthbound.

"Dillon," I announced, the words of which shook him back to life, "this lovely young lady who stands before us is named Aretha. No," I quickly put in before he could say anything, "not Miss Aretha Franklin for unfortunately the Queen Of Soul has, unwisely I would say, decided not to join us tonight, but, in her place, we are very fortunate to be graced by her namesake. So, as my good friend Papa Supino always says, salute!"

"Hi," Aretha said, sitting down and smiling at Dillon. Instantly, I got a little jealous and so I decided to take her whole attention and find out everything about her.

"Are you from London?" I asked, directly looking into her eyes. No? Where are you from? Really? What was that like? When did you move up? As long ago as that. And what do you think of my native town? Yeah, I can dig that. And do you work? For a PR company? Is that what you want to do? Is the money any good? How are the hours? What about your boss? Yeah, they all are. I showered her with a million questions and as she answered I continually looked into her soft blue eyes each and every time, for, to be honest, if she had stood up and thrown a drink in my face, I wouldn't have cared, such was my confidence.

I also found myself edging nearer and nearer to her until the next thing I knew I had slipped my hand into hers and, much to my delight, she gave it a little squeeze and let it rest with her. (Told you so and thank you, Enzo).

Emboldened, I leant over and whispered in her ear, "You know you're the best looking girl here tonight. I really would like to kiss you."

Aretha smiled gently at me for the other notion that came into my mind was that she had dropped one as well. I was convinced of it although God knows where I got that info from.

"Why don't we go and dance first? I want to let off a bit."

"Baby, your wish is my command."

Two minutes later, dry ice swirling around our ankles, I could stand it no longer and reached over, took her waist and pulled her to me. Without shame or any other form of restraint, I kissed her hard and boy-o-boy was that some sensation where you could close your eyes and be aware of nothing but this warm, wet and small creature exploring your mouth while all the noise around you receded into the distance.

It was like being on a merry go round and then my hands were moving into the sides of her dungarees and downwards, for I had genuinely forgotten the numbers around us, when she quickly grabbed them and murmured, "not here." I came to in an instant.

"Sorry," I said, "I'm getting a bit carried away here."

"Yes, you are," she replied, "but it's nice."

"You on one?" I asked. Aretha nodded faintly and then I kissed her again, moving away from her mouth and onto her neck until I felt a pinch on my arm and there was Dillon.

"Easy, you're being watched," he pointed out, nodding to the dancers around us who were smiling at our public indiscretions. Once again, I had totally forgotten Dillon but he didn't seem to mind. He just turned away and started his manic dance, the one that I had witnessed that morning.

I took Aretha's hand and whispered in her ear, "would you like to come back to mine. We can have a smoke and listen to some tunes, if you like."

A look of doubt flashed into her eyes.

"And tomorrow?" she asked, "what happens then?"

"Tomorrow," I grandly announced, "we can go out again," and I meant every last word. "Promise."

"Cub's honour." Aretha gave me a discreet nod and then said, "don't tell your friend, okay?"

"Sure, not a word."

"I'll get my coat and meet you outside."

I went over to Dillon who was now standing by one of the speakers, his eyes closed as he jerked to the music.

"Dillon," I said, "I'm outta here. Early start tomorrow. I've really enjoyed it tonight, it's been great. We should go out more often. I'll bell you at the shop."

And then I hugged him and, believe it, if you had told me that very morning that I would be standing in a house music club embracing Dillon, of all cats, you would have won an awful amount of cashola off me, and that's the truth, Ruth.

But there it was and before I knew it I had made it to the cloakroom, where Aretha was waiting, and she took my hand and up the stairs we went, two at a time, past the security guys and into the cold night air which I greedily gulped at, for it seemed to put me right back on top of the high, and we went in search of a cab.

Removed from the club's noise and chaos, it took me a minute to re-orientate myself and it was then that I caught my reflection in a shop window and I was stopped dead. My hair was all over the shop, my eyes were half closed like a boxers, even though I had perfect vision, and I chewed my gum like a camel, my jaw relentlessly working overtime.

Yet, description above exempted, rarely had I felt this contented with life. As far as I was concerned, the world was as it should be, neat and ordered and without hassle, and as for myself I felt no fear about anything or anyone because in this mood I could take on the worst and come up smelling of roses each and every time. Such confidence is near impossible to find, believe it, for all of us live and breathe our insecurities, battered every day by clouds of doubt and covering up our weak points as best we can. On this shit, such notions don't even come into play and, once again, I wondered why I and everyone else couldn't be this way all the time.

A cab came into view and we hailed it down, and, safely ensconced in the back, holding hands, Aretha asked with a please prove me wrong smile, "I suppose you've got a girlfriend." The word instantly brought Tuesday into my mind. I thought of her at the record fair, and then I was at the hotel room and she was putting her arms around me, but this time, instead of feeling grief or sadness at her vision dancing into my mind, I felt a strange contentment as if I was finally letting a bird out of its cage to fly off into the free beautiful sky.

"No," I said with a smile, "I'm not linked up at all," The next thing my mind brought up was Sandra but, as you can do in a dream, I quickly moved her out of the way, the only real value of her appearance being that it forcefully reminded me I needed some condoms, and that we should stop off at the 7-11 near to where I lived. Directing the cab there, I held Aretha's hand all the way, stroking her fingers and pleasantly coming down now that we were away from the chaos and it was just the two of us anticipating what was to come. I could feel John Thomas twitch everytime I looked over at her dungarees which I intended to remove with the care of a surgeon. It was 3.30 in the morning when I entered the 7-11, telling Aretha I needed sugar and milk. I gave a cheerful, hello-ah! to the extremely bored looking guy behind the counter and made towards the fridge to get some juice. It was there that I ran into my first spot of bother because, without warning, I suddenly became transfixed by all the bright and garish packaged cartons of juice in front of me, a riot of bright words and colour that literally hypnotised me, and if it hadn't have been for the polite couple who waited patiently behind me to grab some milk, I guess I would have been there all night.

As it was, I snapped out of my trance, took out some drinks and, making towards the counter, I noticed the girlie magazines on display which hastened my journey back to Aretha considerably. I went straight up to the counter, and asked for a pack of condoms with a brazen approach I would never have thought was within me. The bemused look on the guy reminded me of the bar woman at the club but I simply didn't care about what he or anyone else, come to that, thought, such was the high. I fished out a fiver so I wouldn't have any problemos with the coinage again, received my change, went back to the cab and we drove back to my yard. In my front room, I put down the drinks, and we eagerly started kissing, only this time Aretha made no fuss as I slid my hands onto her cheeks and pulled her even closer. Then I guided her into the bedroom.

I have to say that sex on E bought out a side to me which I had never experienced before. We literally ravaged each other, lasciviously licking the other's body, both of us ravenous for scent and sensation as we explored each other with a fervour that I wanted to last forever. As we vigourously coupled up I suddenly found myself whispering into her ear all kinds of instructions, demanding she tell me of her fantasies and desires so that we could satisfy each other to the toal max. When she related her story of how she met a stranger on a train and within half an hour they were both locked in the toilet, her on the sink holding on for dear life as he rammed into her, that, people, was the end of phase one. Twenty minutes later, I found myself nuzzling up to her, pushing myself against her side and making signals she could not ignore. Truth be told, phase two was even tougher and dirtier, finding new positions, utilising certain bits of clothing, the lust never wearing off as sensation after sensation came through until, finally, we lay there on my bed, exhausted, sweating, our minds whirring away at a hundred miles an hour, until, unbelievably, John Thomas stirred once more and phase three began. At eight that morning I fell into a light sleep and when I awoke with a start, Aretha had just pulled on her underwear

"I thought I'd just nip out and get some cigarettes," she explained. I got out of bed, encircled my arms around her and began kissing her neck. I moved my hands up to her breasts and massaged them through the thin material. Then I stood back and undid the clasp on her back.

"No," she said, "I'm too tired."

I continued removing her bra and then turned her to face me as I buried myself into her chest, pulling her down onto the bed and not even bothering to remove anything else as I moved her legs apart and entered her. After, we both fell into sleep and when I awoke with a start it was because I was now sober and every part of me was exhausted beyond belief.

"Hi," she said, cheerily.

I just wanted to curl up and drift off into darkness.

"What time is it?" I grunted.

"Two o'clock. What time we going out tonight?"

The words hit me like a sledgehammer. All I wanted was to be solo. I had no words to say to her, nothing to talk about and, people, that is such a horrible sensation to feel towards someone, especially when you've just done the do and made rash promises that you wish your mouth had never uttered. My jaw throbbed badly, my mind was on a true downer and all I wanted was oblivion. As we made polite afternoon conversation, Aretha started to sense my disinterest and although she tried to revive me with numerous cups of coffee, she could see the task was hopeless.

God bless her, though, because, still acting like everything was hunky dory, she placed a little kiss on my cheek as I lay in bed and said, "Perhaps I'll see you next week down the club then," and left. I knew I was in the wrong but my exhaustion outweighed my guilt and I struggled back to sleep. The world had suddenly gone from radiant colour to a very horrible grey and it was only at nine that night, when I stumbled out of bed, did I realise that there was a message for me on the answer machine. It was Sandra.

"Hi. I've decided to go over to Trinidad for a holiday and weigh things up. Whatever I decide will stand. I'll call you when I get back. Laters, loverboy."

Her tone was polite and firm but the message, although I was in no state to realise it at the time, was devastating. Fact is no West Indian goes back to their island for a couple of weeks if they can help it. They stay for as long as possible. By the time Sandra arrived back in the country it would be legally impossible to terminate the baby. She had already made up her mind and she knew it. She was going to have my child. At that precise moment in time I had no inkling of this. All that came into my mind, as I briefly pondered the situation, was the line of a Lennon song my mum used to sing around the house.

It ran, "Nothing's going to change my world," and that for better or worse, was exactly how I felt.

PART TWO

COLOUR ME LOVE

18 MONTHS ON.

This was when I loved up London the most, when the sun blazed down from an azure sky of such staggering beauty that the people seemed to hit the relax mode and lose all their burdens, for even if you held no cashola, which is the biggest drag there is, just to be a character in such an oil painting was a rare treat in itself. That Mary in Brief Encounter certainly hit the spot when she went into one about Britain being so much better to live in if the sun came out and about a lot more, and quite right too, madam, for the heat, like a great massage, loosened up all the glum faces and tight mouths as smoothly as a top burglar picking locks. Invigorated by the disappearance of winter's grey skies, which depressingly blended in with so many of the City's buildings that it made you wonder if the architects of these drab, grey edifices had never been introduced to colour, everyone seemed to re-energise themselves as they were reminded just how beautiful the world can be. It was a welcome respite from the intolerable strain of winter but, even so, there was no getting away from the fact that this heat, which now spread itself so languorously over town, came from a different kind of sun, one that gave off a dry and brittle heat that no one was used to. Apologies for hitting the same riff but there was something slightly disturbing about this relentless heat because that summer, as the sun's harsh rays mingled with the city's fumes, cyclists flashed by with huge pads of cotton wool stuffed in their mouths, a flash of a future that I didn't want to live in, and confirmation that severe adjustments in our way of life would have to be made, no doubt about it, if we were to enter the next decade in some kind of shape. Over at Papa's, in endless cappuccini discussions, Brother P. and I debated the changes that we could sense in the air and tried to make sense of all this shifting scenery, but, unfortunately, and much to our distress, we were constantly interrupted by the raging arguments that erupted every time Papa and his son were within ten yards of each other. Paolo, a good looking 14 year old, who had been blessed with his father's large eyes and his mother's delicate facial features, which was topped off by a lustrous mop of curly, jet black hair, would be sharing a capo with us, his football bag ever present and correct, when Papa would shout over to him, "Eh, the football season is over. Where do you think you're going? Don't you think you should be helping out your famiglia?"

"I'm going training, Papa," the reply would come, Paolo not even bothering to look over to his illustrious padre.

"You're going training? Training on a day like this when we're rushed off our feet, sweating like pigs to put food in front of you. What about doing some training for here? Eh, what about that? One day this will be yours and then what you going to do? Eh! Answer me. And what about me and mama. You ever think about us when you're training? You ever think about us when you're kicking a ball around all day? What is the matter with you?"

"Nothing's wrong with me, Papa, except the father I was given," and then Marissa, who had been carefully clocking the argument, would put down everything and quickly stand between the two of them before it really got out of hand, and tell them to act like grown men instead of bambini.

"Stop it now," she would command as Papa shouted at the top of his voice that his son had no respect, and that he would teach him a lesson, and Paolo responded by turning his back on him even more.

Brother P. and I never intefered, as you can imagine, but I have to say that my votes were with Paolo. To most people, his dream of playing the professional seemed a thousand miles away but, as he always insisted, and quite right too, why shouldn't he realise it? Others had, why not he?

"It's only yourself who stops you in this life," Paolo told us, so bright and clear for a boy of his age.

"Even if I fail, so what? I tried and that's more than most people even attempt. But I'm good enough. I know I am. I feel it.

Here," and he tapped his heart twice with a confidence that was proud and, I have to say, not a little inspiring.

"See," he continued, "I don't know why but I've always been haunted, from an early age, by the thought of getting old and realising that you never did in life what you really wanted to, never even tried it, just thought to yourself, ah, I can't do that and left it at that. A whole life wasted because you talked yourself out of your purpose. That's terrible. Papa doesn't see it because he achieved what he wanted but it's not what I want. It's unfair to force it all on me because I never asked for all this in the first place."

"He's only doing what he thinks is best for you," I put in. but, really there was no need to articulate such a sentiment because Paolo knew that and, despite all the hot words and the raised fists, the stinging insults and the botheration, the fact remained that, deep in their hearts, they loved each other up fully and would always be there for each other if the crunch really came down.

Both knew it but both wanted to prove that love in different ways.

"You wait until I make it, Papa will be so proud," Paolo prophesied. "Don't tell him but a scout has already put in an offer for when I leave school. I was top scorer in the league last year."

"That's great," Brother P. said. "Does Papa know?"

Paolo scowled. "These days, he refuses to come and see me play. I don't think he's seen me on the pitch for two years now."

"The fact of the matter," Paolo continued, picking up his bag and collecting himself up, "is that I will make it, no doubt about it," and, I have to say, it was hard not to be impressed by the boy's utter certainty in himself, for at a tender 14 years of age he already knew where he was going and few people twice his age, possessed that fact. Papa was not impressed with his departing son.

"Marissa," he shouted, "I'm going to see Father Espositio tonight. Perhaps he'll be able to to talk some sense into his stupid head," and he stalked back into the kitchen, leaving me with the thought that maybe I would be better off with the priest's counselling, for the truth of the matter was that Sandra had arrived back from Trinidad some 10 months back, set on course for motherhood.

I had parlared with her on three seperate occasions, the worst time being the first time we met up in mid July, to supposedly discuss if she was going to go ahead with the birth, this meet up taking place in a chainstore pizza parlour. Her stomach had now started to noticeably swell up and, when she finally walked in, after keeping me waiting for twenty minutes, the sight of her condition caused a rumble of rage to go off inside me. I tried to hold it down, bite my tongue and act civil.

"Alright?"

"Alright."

She ordered garlic bread to be followed by ice cream whilst I settled for a cappuccino and, hopefully, the confirmation that she would soon be out of this condition and back to normal.

"How was Trinidad? Your family okay?"

"Oh, I had a great time."

I reached for a cigarette.

"I'd rather you didn't if you don't mind, I've given up."

"Sure." A silence, and then, "So did you come to any decision while you were away?"

"I'm having the baby, our baby. It's too late to stop now even if I wanted to."

"How do you mean?"

"Well you can't get an abortion after 13 weeks."

I felt the ground give way beneath me as it came to me how she had brilliantly bamboozled me.

"You knew before you went away, didn't you? All that stuff

about wanting to think things over. It was bullshit. You tricked me. You fucking well tricked me!"

"Sorry," was all she could say.

I stared at her in complete disbelief.

"Can't you see that I'm not into this at all. Can't you open your eyes and see that. What is wrong with you?"

"I don't care," she coolly replied. "It's my body, my decision. That's it."

"Your body, our baby. Doesn't anything I say mean anything to you? It's like talking to a fucking brick wall. Don't you understand I want nothing to do with this? Can't you see it from my side of things? You'll be bringing it up single handedly. I ain't helping out. I want nothing to do with it. That's it. Final, finito, over and out, lovergirl."

"Why are you so scared of this?" she asked, not even raising her voice but coming like she was an interested doctor trying to coax things out of a wayward patient.

"Why do you run away? Don't you want to see your own child grow up and be a part of it?"

"Look," I said wearily, "we had a thing going for a couple of months, alright? That was it. It was nice while it lasted, and all that good stuff, but all I know is that it didn't go the distance. One of those things and end of story. Now what point is there in prolonging it?"

"So, I'm not good enough to bear your child is what you're saying. I'm okay to fuck for a couple of months but God forbid that I should bring your precious children into this world."

"Did I say that?"

"You don't have to, dear. I know where you're coming from. The slightest problem and that's it, off and running." Sandra gave out a cruel laugh and then sneered at me.

"You men really are something else. You walk around like you own the world and everyone in it. Then something happens that doesn't fit into your little plans. Someone comes along and asks you to, and I really hate to use the word in front of you, take some res-pons-i-bility for your actions and you get shit scared. Pathetic, the lot of you."

"Not as pathetic as bringing unwanted babies into the world."

The waiter had just arrived with the order and so had no idea why the slightly overweight woman he was serving, with one magnificent sweep of her arm, swept away everything he had put on the table, plates, cups, cutlery and food, and sent it all crashing to the floor, the deafening noise silencing the whole joint.

"My baby is not unwanted," Sandra screamed. "You may not want it but this baby that you helped to make is going to get everything in life, whether you're there or not. And don't you ever insult me like that again or I swear on my mother's life I will kill you."

"Not," I said, standing up, "if I kill you first," and then I walked, leaving her crying at the table, ice cream spreading slowly around her feet.

I spoke to Sandra twice after that unhappy occasion and both times the rows erupted like volcanos, and so I simply blanked her. I left the phone on the answer machine, ignored her messages and threats and got on with my life. To be God's honest, and I know this sounds a little jittery, but I was far more interested in what was going on down at my place of employment, The Unity Club, than spending time and effort on this ugly business. For, without warning, the scene I had witnessed, and taken part in, down at that South London venue with Dillon, had been repeated all over the country. It took some time but the acid house kick had taken off in Manchester, Bristol, Leeds, Glasgow, and every other major spot in the country. The combination of house music and ecstasy had proved to be spot on, creating a brand new movement not witnessed since the punk days, and it was only right and proper that in a world where we have to re cycle if we want it to carry on, the scene should be born out of a similar process with the attitude coming off a '60s vibe - peace, love and spirtualism - and the fashion recalling the '70s. It needed a drug to bring it to life and ecstasy fitted the bill perfecto. That small white pill gave you such huge energy, confidence and spirit that it forced you to shed all inhibitions, and in no time at all, the elitist attitude that had pervaded the Capital's clubland for years was gone, as a new breed of clubber came into being and turned the town upside and down.

Populist and addictive, clubs now thrived on a new energy that was electrifying. You would walk into joints and the music would be pounding away whilst the people stood on risers, chairs and tables and let off big time. In the prole parlance of the scene, a lot, and I mean a lot, got right on one matey and let loose some wild stories, that I now must relate.

A regular couple I knew from The Unity, a Greek guy and his English Rose of a gal, were caught by security guards, early one morning, loving it up in the Natural History musuem toilets after a night on the pill.

A fellow DJ was offered a spot at a rave somewhere in the country and, for the first time, dropped an E, to get himself into the spirit of things, just as he reached the secret venue. He hung around the place for a bit and then went back to his car to collect his records. A search party found him an hour later in the back of his four wheeler, record sleeves scattered around him as he lay slumped, actually caressing his tunes and telling them how much he loved them up.

Again, in an after hours illegal joint, many of which had sprung up to cope with the demand for raving all night long, a fully E'd up guy, left the dancefloor in search of a leak. Stumbling into the urinals, he unzipped and commenced to relieve himself, until the screams and laughter of the people around him, informed him that he had not actually left the dancefloor and was now spraying those all around him. At that very club, another guy, eyeing up a particularly enticing Goddess, knelt down in front of her and requested that she spend the rest of her life with him. On receiving a stern refusal, as she played for the other team, he then started following her around on all fours, screaming, "I'm a love struck puppy for you, baby!" until a bouncer came in, picked him up and turfed him out.

Wild times, people, wild times, yet I have to add that this small white pill had other uses as well and made you realise why the powers that be have designated drugs as persona non gratis. Ecstasy not only threw a manic party but it brought with it a certain frame of mind that made people start to question everything around them. Not only relationships but how this country and the world operated, and that's when the greyers start getting nervous. Drink yourself stupid by all means because you'll only wake up with a hangover but start looking into the nature of things and that is the one thing the greyers can't handle.

As for me, myself and I, well, I had to put a brake on swallowing that magic pill for many reasons. To kick off with, it began intefering with my work and ruining all the best laid plans of my carefully constructed mixes. I would forget certain records or play the mix in completely the wrong order. Some nights, I was too boxed to cue the tune up correctly, or I would have to spend the whole night trying to resist the urge to leave my booth and shake it down with the rest of them on the dancefloor. Plus, no one had any true info on the long term affects and I certainly didn't want to carry on dropping until the judgement was in on that particular matter. I mean, it stood to reason that, such was the high it gave you, an experience which had some numbers dropping as many as five in a night, ("five! I've done five!") that there had to be a kickback which I didn't particularly want to stay around and meet.

This world is run on a balance and as that old saying goes,

what go up must come down, and ain't that nothing but the truth. On the occasions that I went AWOL from this world, the big comedown happened and without fail. What's more, it wasn't always the following morning that you hit rock bottom, as you do with other relaxants, but, by and large, the shutters really came down days later as you were overwhelmed by feverish nightmares and a hefty dose of vicious insomnia which kept you up until the morning sun, swearing you would never touch it again.

Six months after it came to these shores, you started bumping into medical scare stories that told of paralysis of the spine or Parkinson's disease, accompanied by smug knowing expressions which lended even more credence to the scenario.

The other matter that bugged me out were the dealers you did business with, particularly those lonely, and for good reason, individuals who would engage you in conversation as part of the payment, when all you wanted to do was hand the cashola over and split.

The next night, sober as a Lord, the pusherman would spot you and make his way over to carry on the talk like you were bosom buddies, whilst you stood there looking for any chance to split. At the time, one of my main regrets was that Brother P. never enlisted in pill service. He wanted nothing to do with the chemical factor and was always quick to remind me that I too was once of this notion.

"Yeah," I would reply, "but we all change. Anyway, it's not like I'm addicted or anything. You should try it for the experience."

"Jesus," he sneered, "you sound like Timothy Leary."

Matters came to a head one night when I dropped a half down at The Unity and, taking a break from my booth, waltzed into the manager's office and belled him with the news that I really dug him and our link together. That very night, at about four in the morning, he showed up at my flat. I was still up, smoking and playing tunes.

"Hey, P. come in."

"No, I won't. I just want to say that if you have anything to say to me, you say it without that shit in your body, fucking your head up. You understand me, boss?" Then he split into the night and I didn't hear from him until three days later, by which time I had resolved to ease off, and told him so, adding an apology.

"Seen," he said and, like the friend he is, never brought it up again. It was this bump, plus another incident, that I will now relate, which truly caused me to ease off.

I had arrived at The Unity for the nightshift one night and, in a slightly reckless mood for I had been dwelling on the Sandra business, checked in my tunes and proceeded to drop an E. J.J., my warm up man still had an hour to go and I figured that by the time I was due on, I would be over the rush that can buckle your knees and leave you speechless, and firin' up on all cylinders.

Swallowing the bitter pill, I made for a dark corner and, sure is sure, twenty minutes later it was lift off time and I was off, feeling groovy, spending the time just checking out the few dancers that had arrived and digging the scene as the music filled my head, and that warm glow suffused my body.

No one paid me any mind until I felt, once more, that magical surge of power and energy take a hold of me. I badly wanted to DJ, now that I was filled with an unstoppable enthusiasm, whose pull I could not resist, and an unquestionable belief that I was the best DJ around, and no one there was to touch me. I felt as if I was walking on the clouds as I made my way to the booth to start playing and, giving J.J. a brief hug, which caused a look of slight shock to cross his face, I pulled out a current fave and true classic, Frankie Knuckles's transcendental "Tears", and mixed it in, aiming to follow it up with Doug Lazy's "Let It Roll."

All the time I had failed to notice the commotion going on at the club's front door, and nor did I see Jill, who had been distinctly cool with me since the Sandra business had kicked off, standing next to me until I felt her tap on my shoulder. When I clocked her my first impulse was to try and clear the air with her, sit her down and tell her my side of the story, but she was not at all interested in what I had to say. She had a far better line to deliver.

"Have you seen who's outside?" she asked and then, a little pause for dramatic timing, "Sandra's here and she's got a baby with her. Looks just like you, loverboy."

I couldn't help it, I laughed out loud.

"Ease off, Jill. I'm working."

"See for yourself."

"Look Jill, I know you're pissed with me but you don't have to go this far."

"I'm not joking. Check it out."

I looked over to the front door, which you can clock from the booth, and saw Charlie, the bouncer, shaking his head and obviously arguing someone. I couldn't believe it was Sandra.

"You're taking the piss, I know you are, Jill."

"Afraid not, sweetheart. It's time to face the action because if you don't go over there and let her in, then I will. Simple as that."

"Look Jill, I know we've had problems..."

"Go to the front door. I think it's you who has got a problem."

I swallowed hard.

"I can't leave here. I'm working."

"I'll get J.J."

Jill went off on a search party and I began trying to compose myself, to search for a normal state of mind, but it was not forthcoming. Fact is, people, I was as high as a kite and with no landing space in view.

Jill returned with J.J. and I made my way to the entrance, wishing to God that there was an exit door I could just disappear into, but, of course, there wasn't one, just Charlie who was using his arm to block Sandra's entrance.

The first thing that caught my attention was the contrast between Charlie's muscular, black arm thrown across the door, and the virgin white of the baby's blanket. In fact, I got so wrapped up digging this particular colour clash, I failed to hear what Charlie had to say on the matter, although his words soon cut through.

"You deaf or something? I said, I'm not letting this woman with that child into the club."

I gazed slowly at Charlie's concerned, tight set face and then at Sandra who, just by the look of extreme determination on her face, told me that it would take a nation of bouncers to stop her.

"It's alright, Charlie. Just let her in for five minutes."

"No way, pal. Absolutely, no way. You might work here but I am not going to be held responsible."

"I'll be responsible," I replied.

Sandra let out a loud tut.

"Cha! The day you show any responsibility will be the day the earth freezes over."

It was a true horrorshow and what compounded the nightmare further was the fact that I was finding it increasingly hard to focus on one person or distinguish their voices. Colour blurred my vision and babble was all around me. I tried to concentrate solely on Charlie.

"Look, Charlie, man, it'll be cool, I'll....." but the words just fizzled out and melted away into thin air. My mind was a blank, all I could see was the virgin white of my baby's wrapping and I could think of nothing to parlare with.

"Look at him," I heard a voice say. "He's off his nut."

"He's on one!"

"Get right on one, matey," came a third laughing voice, and if there's a hell below then this is how it must be, a nightmare chorus of faces and voices screaming with laughter at you, and there you stand, unable to even move a muscle in self defence.

Luckily, in the midst of this terrordrome, Jill had gone to fetch Costello, the manager who, thankfully not checking the condition I was in, and wishing to get the queue moving, instructed Charlie to let Sandra pass. There was a smattering of applause and cheering when Charlie reluctantly moved back his arm, and then came female shouts of encouragement.

"Go for it, sister."

"Tell him how it is, gal."

"Don't take no shit. They're all the same, the wankers. I should know. I married one."

"Shut up, woman. You're the one that said yes."

Costello led us impatiently into his tiny office, which is just inside the entrance to the left, a small space that is dominated by a large desk with papers, coffee mugs, overflowing ashtrays, wrapping paper from the fish shop down the road, strewn all over it.

"Five minutes," he barked. "I'm running a club here not a nursery."

And then, shooting me a glance which did not bode well for my future employment, he made his exit. Sandra turned to me and held the small bundle in her arms up to me. I clocked a small, sleeping, light brown face, with a single wisp of hair falling down the forehead, and realised here, indeed, was my daughter.

"This," Sandra softly said, "is Kimberley. Our baby. I do hope you like the name but as you weren't around after the seven hours it took to bring her into this world, I took the liberty. I hope you don't mind and tough shit if you do."

Sandra started going into one but to be God's honest it was of no consequence for her words, like the sea beating against the rocks in a rage, crashed uselessly against my ears.

All I could do was to stare at this tiny, human form and try and make a link and, cruel as I know this sounds, I found it impossible. I could not check that this was my child for I saw nothing of myself in its sleeping face. She looked like a thousand other babies.

"Of course," I heard Sandra saying as her words suddenly flooded in, "both Kimberley and I are very honoured that you've taken this time to see us. We both know what a busy man Daddy is, don't we baby? Yes, we do and we both really respect your hectic schedule. But don't worry, Kimberley is really into clubbing it, aren't you, darling? Even at this age, all she wants out of life is to DJ. She's got such big ambitions, just like her dad."

Boy -O-Boy did that woman have a tongue on her although her sharp words did help to clear my mind a little.

"Look Sandra, I don't know what you're playing at but I could lose my job here."

"Good. I hope you do. Look at you. You're a disgrace, man. I can't get a penny out of you and here you are out of your head, having the time of your life. How much you pay for whatever it is that's made you look and act like a zombie? Uh? 10 quid? 20 quid? And I'm strugggling to put food into baby's mouth."

A tear involuntarily shot out of her eye and she angrily wiped it away.

"Whether you like it or not this is your daughter and you better wake up to that fact instead of spending time off your stupid face in this poxy club, pretending that everything is cool. It isn't."

"Damm right it isn't," I shot back but she had wounded me badly and I had to admit it. "But if it's dosh you're after I'll start sending some over, okay?"

"Don't be too generous."

"Why don't you just cut this crap and leave, babe. You've got what you wanted."

"Crap? Cut the crap?"

"Yeah, you heard me. Just leave, woman."

"You haven't even met your own daughter, your own flesh and

blood and you talk to me about crap? You should have a look in the mirror, boy, before you start dishing out advice."

By now, the drug inside had weakened, wounded by the fire of her words, and now it went the opposite way as I felt anger swell up inside.

"You don't get it, do you? Haven't you got a brain? How many..."

"Don't shout in front of my baby, if you don't mind."

Behind Sandra I could hear the dull thud of the music thumping through the wall. I imagined the crowd living it up and wished I could be with them, anywhere but here. I took my voice down to a frantic whisper.

"How many times, Sandra, how many times? I don't want this child. It's lovely and great and if you want to go play happy families, then cool. But I'm not coming with you. I've told you I'll give you money but that's it. Just don't bring me into it anymore."

"Don't bring you into it? You put her inside me. You helped make this child, in case you've forgotten. And what do I get? I get shouted at in the street, I had to go through the birth on my own, I'm treated like a fucking leper because you haven't got the guts to face me. You ignore all my calls and then I'm forced to get on a bus and come to this shithole so that you can meet your daughter, who is now seven months old. And you say, don't bring me into it? Sweetheart, it's too late for that business. You're in it. The moment you put yourself inside me you were in it."

"You know your problem, Sandra, you think you're so right and perfect. Oh yes, I'm just off to Trinidad to think about things and when I come back I'll make a decision. Oh my, is that three months gone already? Don't worry. I've only known you for less than three months but, hey, let's bring up a baby. Wouldn't that be nice?"

Before she could respond there was a knock on the door and

there was Costello motioning that enough was enough, and back to work.

"Okay, Mr. Costello. I'll be there in a second."

Sandra laughed out loud. "My, my, so there is someone whose got you on a piece of string. Wonders will never cease."

"Sandra, if I lose my job here you are going to be the first to hear about it. Believe that."

"I came here," she replied with grit, "to tell you one thing and that is if you don't start paying your daughter the attention she deserves, I am not only going to slap you with every court order going but I'll make your life hell. Believe that, loverboy. This is your last chance to get your act together. Our daughter needs a father and if she doesn't get one then I am going to make you wish you had never set your eyes on me."

"Baby, I wish that already."

"Yeah, well let me tell you sweetheart, you never did me one favour, in or out of bed."

With that last stinga, Sandra walked and it was all I could do not to slam my fist down on Costello's table, although, I must add, that I felt a certain relief at her exit for it signalled, I prayed, the end of the nightmare. I returned to the booth and took charge of the dex, sullenly mixing in tunes with a cold shock hanging close over me, Sandra and the sight of our baby cramming my mind at every possible moment. When the lights came mercifully up, I packed up my tunes and, not stopping to parlare with any of the regulars such as The Sherrif or Jasmine, I was outta there and in fast time, let me tell you, heading homeways as my mind's solar system went haywire. The truth was that this was the first time the reality of my actions had been forced upon me and it had cut me to the quick.

They often say that the killer punch is never the sledgehammer blow but the soft one you never saw coming, and Sandra had thrown it beautifully, no doubt about it. To be boxed outta my head and then be forced to confront her and the child, had not only kicked me hard but it also convinced me, there and then as the cab sped Northways, to ease off the white pill. The cashola saved would go to Sandra.

The next night I had arranged to meet up with Dillon and travel southside to a secret rave he had helped organise. I didn't particularly fancy going but as I had given him my word, we met up although I have to say that at the back of mind it was slowly dawning on me that I only really checked for the man either when I was charged up or in his shop, buying up tunes. Outside of that the chit-chat tended to dry up.

The rave was situated in a deserted warehouse and was full of youngsters in loose dungarees, smiley t shirts and wallabee shoes, the uniform of the scene which they all adopted without question, their eyes buggin' and gums working overtime, and I felt little in common with them, no doubt due to the events of the night before and the comedown I was now anticipating with dread.

When Dillon went off in search of a hit, I went wandering listlessly around the club when I bumped into none other than Lord Haw Haw, standing stiffly against a wall and obviously lost in space. I knew he wouldn't recognise me, their sort have people to do that for them, but I hung close by, figuring that my tailor amico, Davey Boy, would be somewhere in the vicinity, a hunch that was proved large and correct.I checked him first.

"Davey Boy, how are things? Cool?"

"Alright there, Mr. DJ. How's tricks or don't you see her anymore? You know William, don't you?"

"Yeah, I think so."

I shook off the notion to doff my hat and bow, and we exchanged polite nods. As you already know my feelings on the subject I will refrain from going into one, although I was somewhat surprised that some 18 months after our first encounter, these two unlikely lads were still hanging close.

"Yes, William and I are in business together," Davey Boy suddenly sprung on me. "We've gone into management. Pop group management. A band from round my way, in fact. Isn't that so, William?"

"Yes," he replied. "I believe they're going to be rather large."

"You're managing a group?"

"Yeah, you know, like the ones you see on telly holding guitars and singing. They're called On One. Top boys if you ask me. Going to be big. Actually," Davey Boy added in a bit of a whisper, "they're a bunch of herberts. Lead singer, if you can call him that, has been on the glue since he was 12 and the drummer's got his case coming up tomorrow. GBH against a British Rail guard. It's the second time this year we've had a night out for him. Last time he got away with a fine. Tomorrow could be different. Do you want to meet them? They're over there."

I followed Davey Boy's finger to a group of young guys, slumped against the wall, staring up at the lights above them and not moving an inch. The psychedelic lights swirled across their young faces, tattooing their skin in such a way that they instantly looked twenty years older. Thin and blank eyed, it was not a pretty sight.

"They're a bit tired, tell you the truth," explained Davey Boy. "Been in a crappy little studio down Hackney all day getting a demo together. Smashing record. "Happy Rave," it's called. This crowd will love it. Right up their street. I'll get you a copy when it's done. I've already got a few record companies sniffing around but I've told them all the same thing. You want to hear the record, fine. Just don't forget your cheque books or you'll be wasting your bus fare, know what I mean?"

"Where does Lord Haw Haw fit in?" I enquired.

"William? Bought all the equipment. Great gear, it is. You can do what you like with it. It's un-be-fucking-lievable some of the stuff. Does everything for you. Push a few buttons and you could have my granny, and she's 89 if she's a day, sounding like Pav-a-fucking-rotti. Just as well really. Those boys couldn't string two fucking notes between them. Fancy an E, by the way. The boys will sell you some. They supply their estate."

"Nah, I'm off that shit."

"Here, I heard you had a bit of trouble last night."

"News travels fast in this town."

"Sounded nasty to me. I mean, call me old fashioned but it's not on is it? Bringing a sprog down to a club. You know what I would have told her? Darling, I don't come and disturb you when you're working at McDonalds, so don't come here and disturb me when I'm working. Still, things will sort themselves out. They always do. By the way, you going to help us out when the record comes out?"

"How do you mean?"

"Give it a few spins down your club, get the hillmans worked up, know what I mean? I can sort you out a nice little tonik number."

"Davey, how long have you been sorting me a nice little tonik number out?"

"I know, I know, but hand on heart I've got a few new contacts in that department. I'll see what I can do. By the way, don't let this baby malarkey get to you, son. You don't look good on it."

The Sandra business was precisely what I had come out to avoid and, knowing Davey's predilection for parlaring endlessly on the same conversation, I switched the talk.

"Lord of the manor don't say much, does he?"

"William? He's just dropped an E. Doesn't know whether he's coming or going. You should stick around for when it gets him dancing. Looks like an ostrich having a shit!"

I don't know how but it suddenly struck me there that Davey Boy's relationship with William might actually go a bit deeper than just management but it was not the kind of thing that you bring up in polite conversation, if it needs to be brought up in the first place, and, despite his entertaining patter, I knew it was time to split.

Homeways was the bestways for there is a time in everybody's runnings when you simply have to disappear from view, take stock of all your inventory, so to speak, and, like a master chess champion, plot out the next moves.

"Davey Boy, I'm gone. Check you soon."

"Alright, sonny boy. Don't forget, they're called On One and they're going to be huge. Ain't that right, William?"

That night as I lay in my yard in a deep Nina, the window flung open and the world silent around me, I looked towards the moon beaming down as if the Lord Above was holding a torch and throwing a light into all our lives, and realised that for the first time since they jumped bail, I truly missed my P&M.

I don't know the runnings you have with your family, but with mine it got to be like sharing a house with two close friends that you could always go to for the words of wisdom that you need from those older than yourself, the ones who have already navigated the deep waters we all find ourselves in, and there they are to point you the right way. In my mind, I couldn't blame them for doing a Houdini but, to be God's honest, in my heart I badly wished they hadn't jumped ship, because right now their little boy blue needed them. Unable to kip, I wandered into the front room with the express intention of playing some tunes when I noticed the answer machine flashing. I pushed the play.

"Yeah, P. here. Heard about last night. If it gets too mad, bell me or try Kind Of Blue by Miles. It helps. Believe it. Go well."

I did just that and awoke on the sofa at about ten the next day, the thought of belling Sandra and the kiddiwink uppermost in my mind. This I did and we made an arrangement to meet but, like St. Peter, three times I failed them, covering my tracks with fake stories of illness or a malfunctioning public transport system.

That terrible night at The Unity had shaken me more than I can say for I still felt a huge grievance aginst her for creating single handedly that nightmare of a scenario which was now all over town, distorted in a rush of whispers. Not showing up was my way of getting back at her although I knew, deep in the heart, that I was just playing for time, clinging fast to my world which was now spinning faster than ever I wanted it to.

Luckily, beautiful summer had really kicked in by now, covering this boss city and its inhabitants in a warm, hypnotic haze, and, when you woke up and saw that glimpse of blue sky through the crack of the curtains, you could not help but be inspired to get busy. Summer that year was special and it threw up two tunes that will always take me back, when I hear them, to those days, that bitter-sweet time when I lost my youth and had no idea where to find it. Everywhere I reached, those tunes seemed to follow me, thumping out of shop doorways, open car windows, council blocks, radios and any club you ventured into.

One of them was Public Enemy's "Fight The Power", perhaps the best rap tune yet to be concoted in that cauldron they call New York City, a lethal, charged up tune that was every bit as vital as the film, Do The Right Thing, it appeared in.

When the group's leader, Chuck D., literally pulled down one of the white west's biggest statues with the lines, "Elvis was a hero to most/But you know he didn't mean shit me," everyone in the know, didn't matter what colour, felt the power of the new breed. It was a call to arms, a declaration of war against the old guard who control the strings, and it felt like the birth of a new nation.

The other tune that dominated the summer was Soul 11 Soul's "Back To Life," the breakthrough sound of a funky, street spirtuality that was far too black for the union jack and the best example yet of the New Briton's creative powers. Brothers and sisters, I don't know what the world is coming to but I have to let you know how I loved up those tunes. They fired up and caught in motion a new optimism, because, soon enough, everyone you met was onto something, such as making records, scripting films, designing clothes, starting up magazines, and all with the attitude that no longer were people prepared to wait around for those with the cashola to take note of their talents. Ideas came together and the people linked up to sow the seeds of a cultural revolution.

That summer anything and everything seemed possible, the promise of potential filled the air and I responded by going and doing the one thing that nobody, least of all me, myself and I, thought possible. I fell in love. Chickaboo and Chickabee, I had not planned for this latest development and how could I? Love is the most unpredictable element there is, always striking when you least expect, and so when it hits, all you can do is close your eyes and hope and pray that the journey you are about to undertake is a fruitful one.

As you know, I had traversed this road before with Tuesday and, after being led into an emotional maze of hurt and pain, had no desire whatsoever to repeat the experience, and can you blame me? What I didn't know was that you can only run against the flow for so long, so consider, if you will, the following plotline, which not even a top Hollyweird writer would dare submit, which, before I knew it, had led me back to love.

Early one Saturday evening, two hours before I was due to check in at The Unity with the Brother P. in tow, I recieved a call from an agitated Costello, asking me not to reach that night. A disgruntled customer who had been forcefully ejected by Charlie for caveman behaviour, the night before, had returned to the club in the dawn hours and exacted his revenge by starting a small fire outside the front door. Although the flames had not licked up too much, the damage was enough for the local powers that be to insist that the club close for the night, until the neccessary could be done to it. I belled the Brother P. with the news and we both agreed to take a breather and both stay in that night, agreeing to check each other later on that week. I sorted out my tunes and began cleaning up my yard when at 10.45 p.m, a hunger pang forced me out onto the Stroud Green and, there I was, heading towards Bee Wee's for a chicken roti and rice, passing all the citizens who stood outside pubs in the warm night air, shooting the breeze for all to hear, and very pleasant it was too.

I reached the small restaurant, passed my order to Sam, the genial proprietor and waited on. Just as my food arrived, the door swung open and there, before me, was Little Scissors Jackie, a local gal I know from the hairdressers, hence her title, out and about with her possee. I am on good speaking terms with this gal thanks to the bargain we struck up when I landed my position at The Unity, the details of this agreement being that whenever she wishes to pass by The Unity she does so for nada, whilst, in return, my hair is cut and styled for the very reasonable price of absolutely nothing, and you can't say fairer than that, Jack. I am always pleased to check the gal because she is one number who always seems to exhude positivity, that is life's downs never seem to throw her off track.

"Hey, Jackie," I said to her, "where are you blowing tonight."

"Down southside for a small rave. Fancy it?"

In that no nonsense way this happy band of female numbers bade follow me to a party in Putney that was being held in some friend of theirs house, and, on the spur I agreed, and glad I was too for it was a firin' little affair with cool people and sounds to take up my interest all night.

Then, as the sun once again began to rise over the metropolis, Little Scissors Jackie insist we pack into her car and head for Clapham Common, for this patch of land was now a meeting point for ravers from all over the country to come and rest up after a hard night out on it. We reached the common around 6.30, set up shop and then I dozed off with the touch of the sun's rays like a balm upon my skin, and when I finally came to, about three hours later, it was to discover that the night's posse had been expanded by one.

The gal in question was a friend of Little Jackie's named Indigo. She had passed by as I lay asleep and was now laid out, reading a book. Here's the rub. The book, Nelson George's Death Of Rhythm and Blues, was mine, the tome reaching her doorstep, like the Olympic torch being passed on, by the following route. Brother P., who I first lent it to, then onto his sister, Amanda, who, in turn, gave it to a friend, none other than Indigo. I knew the book was my copy because, back in the days, I had passed through a bookshop where the author was holding a sign in and had him scribble his name on the cover, this writer, a New York boy through and through, being one of the very few to cover my musical beat with style and wisdom.

Apart from the fact that you have to be careful when you lend your things out, as JB once said, outta sight, outta mind, I had to wonder at the coincidence of it all and what it all meant. I was soon to find out. That book gave Indigo and I not only a topic of conversation to keep us busy for the next hour as we argued the why's and wherefore's of the author's theories, but acted as a constant reminder of life's simple twists of fate.

Indigo, as the name suggests, hailed from a mixed blood background that united Spain with Jamaica, which is why when we began parlaring I was confronted with the prettiest eyes you would care to melt into. Her colour was light brown and she kept her hair close cropped, highlighting a natural facial beauty that no make up could ever enhance. But it was beneath the skin that the true flower of her beauty lived and breathed, because it soon became apparent, as we made with the words, that Indigo was not one to play on her physical beauty, reason being that to her way of thinking there were more important things on earth to consider than a vanity fair.

Sensing the vibe that was coming off between us, Little Scissors Jackie collected up her little gal troops and moved off, leaving Indigo and I to bask in the sun, check out the people around us, and keep a wary eye on the lawmen who were now patrolling the common's perimeters in comically, over subscribed numbers.

"A large group of people who want nothing more than to chill, play music and hang out," I said, "and they're acting like they're about to prepare for war. What's the problem?"

Indigo shifted her body to look over at them. "The media," she replied, shading her eyes from the sun. "Ever since that stuff went into the papers about wild clubs and pill popping, the orders must have come down, be seen to do something about it. The eyes of a nation are upon them," she ended up saying in a mock Winston Churchill voice.

"Anyway," she continued, "large peaceful crowds such as these worry them. Doesn't fit in with the roles they've given us all. Upsets all their training."

Such depressing observations aside, it was a great day, spent, with thousands of other like minded folk, relaxin to the max, soaking up the rays and Indigo and I not at all worried about impressing each other, which, I discovered, is actually the best way to impress, if you get my meaning. As the sun rose high and then started to dip, a coloured and colourful assortment of numbers drifted gently by, or set up base next to us, offering out food and water supplies to all those nearby. Scattered all around us were small radios, all of them tuned to a pirate radio station over the Eastside, which constantly pumped out the best of the day's music - Mondee Oliver, Doug Lazy, Ten City, Blaze, Phase 11 - interspersing the music with cryptic messages such as, "Billy, if you're listening, come over, the milkman has just left..." and sending out news of the raves that had been busted and exhorting all to come down to the common and hang out.

No doubt about it, there was a sense of community here a

feeling that whatever vibe tribe you hailed from, whatever your colours, it didn't matter. I had never witnessed such camaraderie amongst my generation and I couldn't help but idly wonder what it would take for the lot of us to rise up as one and fight the greyers that be, smashing down all their restrictions and hypocrisy in one great swoop. The problemo with such a scenario is that the English are not a race for change and the only way you'll probably ever get a full blooded revolution is to close the pubs down forever. Now that would cause a rumble. At about four that afternoon, I couldn't help but note an extremely fine gal, in shorts and a t-shirt that loosely covered a pair of breasts that would interest men for years, pass by. As I was checking her out, I felt Indigo whisper into my ear, in a leering voice, "Cor, nice pair of tits, eh?" The gal had caught me on the hop and I blushed a little, not something I do everyday.

"Not to my taste, Indigo," I lied but my tormenter was not so easily put off. "What is then?"

Resisting the obvious reply, which would pertain to her very good self, I checked the field of play and rested my gaze on a Latino type gal, sunbathing in a swimsuit with nothing more than a walkman for a companion.

"Yeah, not too bad," Indigo replied, which, I have to say, came as something of a suprise for it is not everyday that a gal gives her opinion on another's charms. "She's got a good body but my choice would have been....him."

She discreetly nodded to a long, curly haired white guy, a very unfortunate creation that can best be described as an unfortunate accident between Bob Dylan and Art Garfunkel, sitting in just his shorts, toking on a spliff and lost in a world of his own drug taking.

"Now that's a bit of alright, don't you think?"

"You must be joking. He's a class A lonely wanker."

"A what?"

"Myself and a close friend," I explained, "have a theory that everyone in this world is a lonely wanker and life is all about what degree you live at. It's our way of acknowledging Jean Paul Sartre without having to wade through his tedious books."

"Oh yes," Indigo replied. "And what degree of lonely wankerdom do you inhabit?"

"About 30 to 40 % I would like to think, and that's a very reasonable level. Certainly less than your Adonis. He's well up in the 90s on the lonely wanker scale, if you ask me."

"Really. Watch him for a minute."

I put the eye on him just as the dreamboat in shorts that I had spotted earlier, returned with two drinks in her hand, one for her and one for...him. He took a swig from the bottle, pulled her down to the ground and there they lay, loving it up all afternoon.

"I think the lonely wanker just got busy," laughed Indigo and returned to her book. But I was not to be put off.

"What you have just witnessed," I explained, "is the Gimp theory in full effect. Developed between myself and Amanda's brother, this is a theory whose main law states unequivocally that the more beautiful the Mary, the uglier the man."

"And why is it," Indigo demanded, "that all the best looking Marys, as you call them, go for these types and not hunks such as yourself and your friend?"

"One, because they have the bottle to approach good looking women because they've got nothing to lose. Two, they have money or a flash motor and three...."

"Perhaps the women like their characters and love them for themselves," Indigo interjected, "and not all the superficial shit."

"Hadn't thought of that one," I confessed.

"I'm surprised at that," she retorted. "You don't seem like the kind of guy who would judge a person on the colour of their skin."

"Most definitely not, madam."

"Then why judge them on the condition of their skin?"

"Game, set and match to you," I had to concede but Indigo was not finished and far from it.

"Women don't see the world the way you men do. You lot, I'm sorry to say, think with your dicks all the time. You do! It's true, I tell you. You ask most men and they'll tell you that the first time they meet a woman one of their first thoughts is, would I sleep with her? True or false?"

"True-ish."

"True or false?" she repeated.

"More true than false."

"It's not completely your fault. Nature demands that you reproduce. Unfortunately, she totally forgot that inteferes with your mind power."

"James Brown," I said.

"What?"

"James Brown. Godfather of soul. He cut a tune called 'Mind Power.' One of his best actually."

She totally ignored me and carried on.

"And if we're going to get on then you're going have to stretch your brains a bit further than just your trousers, if you get my meaning."

Such direct words and attitude, I have to tell, I really dig in women, and the warmth I had instantly felt for Indigo that morning when we met, now turned to hot.

The obvious retort to all her theories was to go personal and ask her if that's what she figured about me, I mean, the thought of sleeping with her was uppermost in my mind when we met. But it's best, on certain occasions, not to say a thing, for some matters are best left unsaid, and that very silence can say more than words ever can.

As the sun started to disappear and the air dropped to cold, we agreed to collect up our things and make our way to the tube.

Picking our way through the crowd, it was one of those crucial moments when you both know you're going to go your separate ways and if one of you doesn't make a move, you might be lost to each other forever.

Deep breath then, and, "Indigo, I've really enjoyed your company today. Is it cool to call you sometime?"

"I was going to ask you exactly the same thing," she replied, and, people, my heart hit that bass line we all know, boom-boom-boom, so loudly that I thought everyone in a ten mile radius would hear it.

Indigo and I wandered off to the tube, her to go eastside, me over to Westward Ho to meet up with the Brother P. as we were going to check, for the second time, Spike's "Do The Right Thing," and so, after exchanging numbers, I made my way to the cinema in an excited, dreamy daze. Truth to say, I could hardly concentrate on the images that flickered in front of me because everytime I looked up at the screen all I could see was Indigo. Later on, at Bar Italia, (Papa's is closed on a Sunday), Brother P. tried to engage me on the film's merits, but it was all to no avail. My solar system could only revolve around one thing.

"P., this is the one, I'm telling you. This gal is fly."

"Yeah? You back on those pills?"

"Easy, you know I've knocked them on the head."

"I've seen her around with Amanda. Yes is all I can say."

"Do you think I should phone her or let her phone me? I don't want to appear too eager."

Brother P. let off a small grin.

"The bells will ring," he said, "the bells will ring."

Indeed they did and a week later, over at my yard, we fell into each other and it went off with such passion and care that it was like we were made for each other from day one.

Afterwards, we lay on the bed listening to Lee Morgan's "Search For The New Land," and, as a wind so gentle and cooling that it must have been the breath of Isis herself softly blew over us, tears unexpectedly started to fall down Indigo's cheek.

I pulled her close and kissed them away.

"What's up, baby?"

"I don't want this to be a one off," she gently confessed, "I've made mistakes in the past that I couldn't stand again."

I pulled her even closer and Indigo told me of her last encounter, how she had kept this guy at bay for months until she was convinced he was cool but serious. They made it and two days later, Indigo called him and a gal answered the phone.

"Might have been his sister or someone," I pointed out.

"Sisters don't tell their brother's girlfriend to leave their husband alone, or die," she simply said.

"Indigo, it's alright, there are no sisters in my life. Believe that."

Checking it now I see that Indigo developed an honesty between us that I had no idea could exist between guy and gal. Indigo knew about men but, unlike others, she didn't pretend it was otherwise. She encouraged me to tell her of gals I had a passing fancy for and she did the same on the guy front. Sometimes, we would sit on a park bench and watch the passer bys, commentating on their appeal or if we were travelling by tube to some destination we would exchange secret nods and winks at certain, unsuspecting individuals.

In our little games, for Indigo was straight on one point and that was if I wanted to go with another, then cool but don't come back to her space, we killed that terrible suspicion which can poison the lover's link. That is, she made me see the pitfall of trying to cover up aspects of your real character that you think the other will dislike, a trap which we all fall into.

"Everyone looks at other people," she once told me, "so just because I'm with you doesn't mean that is going to stop. Not that I'll do anything about it but it's a part of me. The same goes for you."

I fell in even deeper into her world. I don't know if you've ever fallen in love, but I hope you have because it is truly one of life's best highs. For weeks on end nothing, but absolutely nothing, matters except the person you want to be with.

Fact is, when love hits you and hits you hard, it's like entering an altered state where your world and everything in it, is turned gloriously upside down. In your mind's eye all you can fix on is that person alone, and nothing else, at the time, matters. Your every thought is coloured by love, and all your normal runnings, literally fall by the wayside. You know how much my work means to me, yet if it meant having to miss a night at The Unity to be with Indigo, then there was no choice whatsoever, I would be there by her side.

When, on the nights, she was at one of her study classes and then off to home alone, I would shape my hours around her, making tapes up with music such as Marvin's "I Want You" or Roy Ayers's "You Send Me," all the time marvelling at my own sentimentality but always safe in the knowledge that Indigo would accept these gifts with a warmth that ignited my heart. I even tried to write her a couple of poems but when I read them out to Brother P. over the phone his initial silence, followed by a "Yeah, that's...nice," was all the criticism I needed. I binned them.

Living in this delicious haze, I savoured every moment as I forgot the world until, as it had to, it came crashing back in one night when Indigo and I were at my yard, checking out a film I insisted she see, this being a mad Harvey Keitel flick entitled, Fingers.

In the flick, Keitel is a classical pianist with a Mafia man for a dad, and a penchant for walking around New York with his ghettoblaster playing at the highest decibel possible. It had just got to the point where he really coats a guy off in the restaurant for asking him to please turn the music down, ("Turn it down? Don't you know who this is? This is fucking Frankie Valli and

The Four Seasons, mutha...") when the phone rang.

"Yep."

"I got the money. Thanks. Now when are you going to see Kimberly?"

I froze in space and time for, truth be told, I had kept back, from day one, news of the Sandra business from Indigo, scared it might frighten her away. I mean, to have a kiddiwink on your CV is hardly the best way to impress someone, and even though we had established an honesty vibe, I had compounded matters even further, by telling Indigo, when the subject arose, that I had no time or space for bambinos. Luckily, Indigo did not dig clubs so she never accompanied me to The Unity where, no doubt, someone would have informed her of my run in with Sandra, and as she also moved in an entirely different circle of people to me, my runnings were not publicly known. I kept meaning to make amends for this re-arrangement of the facts but, somehow, tomorrow never comes, and so I never parlared on the matter again, prefering instead to spend our nights together rubbing cocoa creme into Indigo's rich body whilst Jazzie B.'s beats and melodies played in the background.

"Soon," I said, "soon."

Indigo glanced over at me.

"It'll be her birthday in a couple of months. You know that, don't you?"

"Yep."

"So?"

I felt a flush come to my face and prayed that Indigo could not hear her voice or my fumbling words.

"Yeah, we'll do something."

"Really?"

"Yeah, it'll be cool. Look, I've got to go."

"Ain't that a surprise."

"Sorry, but I do. We'll talk soon."

"Thanks for the offer."

"I'll call next week."

"Yeah and the Pope's a protestant."

The phone went dead and I swallowed hard.

"Who was that?" Indigo asked.

"Jill from the club. She wanted to know if I'd DJ at some party they're having."

"Oh," replied Indigo and went back to the film which by now had no interest for me whatsoever. I knew I would have to come clean soon but I didn't want to upset the idyllic time we were sharing, for the fact of the matter was that, Sandra aside, everything was coming my way. I had my girl, who gave me the strength of a gospel choir going full tilt, and I had my spot at The Unity Club, which on the nights I spun there, would be rammed with faces and characters of intrigue and interest, the summer sun making them even more agreeable to raving the night away and the spirit of the time bringing each and every one closer together.

Take for instance, Jasmine, an Anglo Indian gal with her dark flashing eyes, petite figure and jet black shining hair. Jasmine was a ball of energy, never able to fully relax but always on the move, and forever bringing back the conversation round to sex, a trait that always ensured that, loitering in her radius, there would be two or three guys, hoping to cash in and get busy with her. Naturally, it took them some time to realise that despite all her bluster, it was not the casual she was after but the very opposite, and so when they approached her with various offers, they were always slightly shocked when they got a kickback.

"You?" you would hear her say to some poor unsuspecting soul, who was whispering in her ear. "I'd rather go home with the dustman, mate."

Jasmine had been kicked out of home at 16 for refusing to take part in the arranged marriage that her parents had tried to foist on her, and so she had been forced to make her way in a world that her people had sought to protect her from. Caught in a twilight world of cultures, where the strictness and traditions of her upbringing clashed with the society she now lived in, Jasmine covered up the confusion as best she could.

Sometimes after a night at The Unity, a few of us would head back to Jasmine's yard and, on certain occasions, she spoke of her P&M with such venom that you knew, deep down inside, that what she really craved was a truce to be established with them, based on mutual respect and some kind of understanding.

Of course, Jasmine would never admit to these feelings but it always puzzled me, myself and I how people, such as her folks, could commit all their lives to a religion that told them to walk in peace and love, and then, in the name of that very religion, they blow precisely the opposite way by outcasting their own flesh and blood. Such actions escaped me but then I was always being surprised by the problemos and worries that you find in people once you cut through their smiling faces, so much so, in fact, that I eventually had to reason that we were all living in our personal world, not the world, and it was a wonder that somehow we didn't all collide into each other at the same time and go off with a huge bang.

What a pic that would have made, especially if you include the persona of another Unity regular, The Sherrif, in the frame. This was a number who had set himself on a direct collision course with anyone who tried to block his path, his excuse being that at a very early age, he had been set upon by a group of coppers, "bunch of freemasons freeloading on me," he snarled, for no reason at all, and had been, he claimed, irrevocably damaged beyond repair.

The Sherif's name derived from his unerring ability to walk into anyplace at anytime and turn it, within five minutes, into something resembling a wild west saloon, with punches, bottles, chairs and tables, flying through the air with the greatest of ease.

The Sherif was a hustler of considerable charm when it came to the gals and it was his strikingly good looks that helped him in this department.

Once in a while he would deign to be photographed for some trendy advertising campaign and for a whole week you would walk around town and not be able to avoid his unblemished face staring belligerently out at you from some poster or other. He was also the bearer of a violent, angry streak which he wisely, said some, foolishly, said others, tended to direct against all authority figures, and as he spent a lot of time in clubs, these tended to be security guards, such as Charlie, who, for The Sherif, represented the worst aspect of the New Briton. "I've been reading George Orwell," he would announce, "and he believes that the English are a nation of shopkeepers. Well he's wrong. They're a nation of bouncers, mean, petty, narrowminded idiots who will never let you in for nothing."

The Sherif gave his signature away every two weeks at the local dole office, so the cashola flow was always a major problemo for him but, recently, he had hit a silver streak and moved himself and his runnings into a Notting Hill pad, courtesy, he informed of us, of a middle aged, rich German lady he was forever promising to show off at The Unity but never quite did.

They had met, he informed us, at a Soho coffee bar where, after a hard day's shopping, the lady in question was resting, and after the introductions were through, he had then taken her on a sight seeing tour of London. Then it was back to the apartment she kept in Notting Hill for a night of champagne and canoodling that proved so satisfying to both partners, that The Sheriff, by early morning, had persuaded her to let him take over the yard so that every time she passed through the Capital, he would be waiting for her, ready and willing to pay his share of the rent, so to speak.

This being his story, and as one couldn't prove or disprove

either way, one had to go with it although, as in the coppers who beat up on him, it always seemed that he too lived in a world where fact and fiction were hard to seperate. Like Jasmine, his words shot out like a crazy waterfall, splashing everyone within range, and it was this gift of verbal dexterity that attracted the people to him, gathering round, as they did, like children, eager for their bedtime story. A sample of an example, his opening line would be something like, "I woke up this morning in Manchester. You ever been there? You should go, they've got some great congo players up there. Anyway, I went up there to check this Tasmanian princess I nearly married years ago but couldn't because she wanted children and I wanted to write poetry. So we argued again and that depressed me too much, so I hopped the train for London and met up with some gangsters who run Soho. They offered me a job but I had to turn them down as my landlady was coming into town for an hour. She was swopping planes down at Gatwick, so I went and met her, took her into the toilet and sucked her little finger for an hour and then bade her goodbye until the next time. By the way, what's the first thing you think about in the morning?"

Things got even more tangled up two weeks later when Charlie, the bouncer, handed in his notice to go and protect a high flying pop star, setting out on tour, from all the screaming kiddiwinks. Learning of this, Jasmine approached me one night, and, after the usual salvo of innuendo, "I see you've got your twelve inchers out...", informed me that Rajan, her brother, had also flown the nest and was there a possibility that he take Charlie's position just until he could find his bearings?

According to the CV on her brother, he was a health fanatic, well versed in martial artistry and although he didn't have Charlie's bulk, he was not a boy to fool with. I told her that I thought it a fine idea but that one thing worried me and put my mind into anxious mode.

Both Jasmine and The Sherif were links of mine and, unfortunately, it was odds on that at some point, The Sherif, given his penchant for goading bouncers, would no doubt take a swing at Rajan and, pardon me, but I could not be responsible for such an occurence, especially as it placed me square in the middle.

Jasmine gave me a sweet smile and told me not to worry my old grey matter on such a thing. That particular scenario, she mysteriously added, had already been sorted, so please, could I at least approach Costello with the idea. This I did and two weeks later, Rajan came to work, decked out in a turban and a tracksuit, he too caught between his family and the new world they inhabited. He made for a fine bouncer, meaning that he didn't hold a grudge against the people trying to get into the club, but treated everyone with a firm courtesy. What was more suprising was The Sherif's attitude towards him who, in a remarkable scene, actually allowed Rajan to frisk him, the first time ever I saw another man's hands near him, without the gory sight of blood and bruises following. I couldn't get a hold on The Sherif's accomodating mood swing towards Rajan until, one night, Brother P., after some close observation, informed me that he wouldn't be at all suprised if Jasmine and The Sherif were getting it on, hence the biting of lips all round. My man's hunch was on the ball and, I figured, made sense. Both numbers were burdened down by their past and maybe together they could at least off load some of the weight and find peaceful contentment. Some hope. Two months after the fling begun, two months in which both had quietened down considerably, Jasmine, arrived, unannounced at The Sherif's Notting Hill pad, to find him entwined in the arms of his landlady. As The Sherif had informed her that the gaff belonged to his sister, Jasmine not only screamed betrayal but incest as well, before rushing down to The Unity where she downed, her head turned upside down, three whiskies, four beers and two large spliffs. Then she waited.

An hour later, The Sherif walked in looking for her. A pint of beer being thrown into his face, a barrage of obscenities that I hesistate to record and a right hook from Jasmine that Ali himself would have been proud of, left him standing motionless, beer and blood dripping down his handsome visage.

The Sherif turned calmly around, walked back to the front door, tapped Rajan on the shoulder, said, "don't you ever frisk me again," and went to punch him.

Rajan, quicker than an arrow, saw the blow coming, ducked and then dragged The Sherif out into the street and administered a series of punches and kicks that had an ambulance screaming up to the club ten minutes later to cart The Sherif off to the emergency ward.

I didn't see the man again for two weeks although this amount of time was nothing compared to an incident, back in the days, when he was forced to spend double that amount in a hospital bed, following his mission to meet Prince and ask him a question that he badly needed an answer to. On tour in London, it was easy to establish on the grapevine that after each show, Prince would head for a small club to deliver an impromptu performance and, although you needed a special ticket to gain entry, and security was tighter than Fort Knox, it was precisely those sort of odds that served to inspire The Sherif even further. At the stroke of midnight, at a northside club, The Sherif bowled up.

"Ticket mate," said the security man.

"Left it at home."

"Well, fuck off back there and get it."

"Eat shit. I'm going in to see Prince. He's expecting me. We have an appointment. Alright?"

"Don't joke with me, son."

"Look dad, you haven't got the capacity to understand one of my jokes, even if it came up stark bollock naked and landed on your ugly face. Now move aside."

"I'm warning you."

"I'm shivering with fright."

"Okay, then, I've tried reason. Now try this."

At which point, the crowd scattered as the security man's fisticuff landed square on The Sherif's jaw, sending teeth, blood and his body clattering to the ground.

The Sherif shook himself to and disappeared, and the crowd, shocked and shaken, started to regroup as the bouncers tried to calm everyone down. Some semblance of normality was just starting to return when suddenly a war cry went up and there was The Sherif, dustbin lid in hand, bum rushing the show.

This time the bouncers didn't wait around to exchange pleasantries, because, boy-o-boy, they started in on him seriously. Bouncers spend the night at a door coiled up and waiting for trouble. When it arrives, all that pent up energy is released and that is not a sight to behold at anytime.

It was as The Sherif was literally fighting off this ferocity, that a black limo pulled up and none other than Prince himself stepped out, surrounded by his bodyguards. Despite his predicament, The Sherif saw his chance to ask the music man the question that had bugged him for so long.

"Prince!" shouted The Sherif, as the bouncers were momentarily stopped by his unexpected presence, "what key is "Sign Of The Times" in? I need to know, me and my mate have been trying to work it out."

But the music man did not stay to answer and The Sherif was hospitalised for a month, a time I was reliably told, he spent composing poems, one of which, 'Kerouac meets The Supremes,' he showed to me on his return to The Unity and, impressed I was too, especially by the opening line that ran, "My pen is as a restless vulture that picks at the corpse of my memory," and told me, at least, that underneath it all, he was not a man to be underrated.

"Why, you should turn your anger to literature," I informed him one night standing up at the booth. He was just about to reply when Stinga appeared and, as this character was now seeing Jasmine, The Sherif was not too enamoured by his presence, although he knew that he had no cause to complain about the failure of his link with her. "Excuse me," he said, "but I must go drown my sorrow in tomato and lemonade juice," and with that he exited. Stinga shrugged his shoulders. "Not my fault," he mumbled.

"Sorry?" I said, trying to make sense although with Stinga that was always a problem. His angle on life was one of the strangest I've ever come across and relates back to Jesus and his 12 disciples. Stinga's belief was that down the ages, certain people had arrived on earth who were also disciples.

His list numbered such cats as Muhammad Ali, Mikhail Gorbachev, Mandela, Stevie Wonder, et al. Therefore, went his reasoning, which was delivered, by the way, with absolute sincerity, through adopting their particular look for a month at a time, he would actually get close to God. Tonight, he was Thelonious Monk, sporting a dark suit, large Russian style hat, and shades, whilst fully indulging in the Monk's supposed habit of mumbling his words. He was also taking piano lessons though one shuddered to think how he would carry off Gorbachev when the time came. Jasmine, who had now come up to the booth as well, felt the same way.

"These gears are alright," she said, "but I'm gone when you get to Gandhi. I mean, are you really going to walk around with round spectacles and a bedsheet? Anyway, bedsheets can be put to much better purposes, know what I'm saying?"

Stinga mumbled a reply and the pair walked off as I pulled out The Night Writers "Let The Music Use You," an awesome, let me tell you, production and song, and started pondering, as I cued it in, on how I was going to break the Sandra news to Indigo. It was a tricky one because either I laid my cards on the table and owned up to her, which might mean her walking on two counts of deception and perjury, or she would find out for herself, and that, my friends, was the whole problemo. Brother P. had advised the first course.

"You talk about this honesty vibe you have between you," he would point out with typical accuracy, "but you haven't told her you're a father? Shit man, you going to have to do better."

"I knows, I knows," I would say, "but I should have told her first time ever I saw her face. Now I feel that if I let the rabbit out, she's going to think that everything I've told her is a crock."

"Man, just tell her. If things are as strong as you say, then it will play, no doubt about it."

The Brother P. was right. Life gives us many things but what it never allows us to do is turn back the hands of time, always a cause of eternal regret, and so I kept my counsel for the time being, and decided to wait for the right moment to arrive.

As I was doing so, the clear summer sky started carrying the scars of approaching autumn clouds, and it was as the season started to make its move, that a letter from Costello, of all people, landed on my doormat. Addressed to all Unity staff, it asked that we attend his office at four in the afternoon, that very day. After a trip Westward Ho to buy up some new tunes and shoot the breeze with whoever was hanging out down at Dillon's shop, I made my way to The Unity, me, myself and I being the last to reach. It was strange, I have to say, to see the club in full daylight, as it transformed it into a place that was slightly unfamiliar.

"Ah, glad you could make it," Costello said, as I made with the apologies and sat down with the rest of the staff on the tables and chairs by the bar. The mood was downbeat and downcast because, unknown to me, certain rumours had been flying around which did not point to a rosy future, a point Costello was able to confirm.

"I have some very bad news," he started and everyone now knew the worst was on its way. "The local council wish to terminate the club's licence and close it down. They wish to build a car park. I am very sad to tell you this but the matter has been voted on and, according to my solicitor, is final and binding."

All of us stared dumb founded at this middle aged Greek guy who, despite all the bluff exterior was, when all was said and done, a decent man to be your wage payer, but at this moment, he looked sad and tired, as if all the years of his life had finally broken through onto his face and shoulders, and beaten him down and into submission.

"I am currently looking for new premises but as this for place..." Costello waved his hand vaguely around him and sat down. He had nothing more to say. The club he had run for seven years was like a second home to him and now the town's planners had taken it away from him. All his memories were to be crushed into the ground by the builder's machinery and there would be nothing left.

One of the staff, a young gal from Bristol called Kathy, who had come up to town to study hard during the day and earn some much needed cashola at night, was not about to stand for it. She shot up and demanded that we organise a petition, to be signed by all the regulars and ourselves, and then follow up with a march on the town hall.

Most people present shook their heads. Either they were not at all fazed by Costello's tragic news or they simply didn't believe, as was the country's present mood, in the value of protest, a concept that Mrs T. had successfully implanted in most people's minds.

"So what do you say?" Kathy demanded of the assembled. There was nothing but silence to answer her.

"What is this?" she asked, puzzled by her silent work companions. "Doesn't anyone want to do something? Are we going to just sit back and let them get away with it?"

She had a fighting spirit that life had not been able to budge, and she also had a point that couldn't be denied, which was namely that if everyone always went with the greyer's demands, then gals, for example, wouldn't have the vote and the Vietnam war would probably still be in full swing.

Costello was not in a fighting mood. "These people," he said wearily, "have made up their minds. All this area is to be turned into a shopping centre. It's wrong and, yes, we can protest but, believe me, they'll do what they want to do. There's too much money at stake. I'll just have to find another club."

"Don't say that," Kathy implored, "don't give up without at least a fight. I know things look bleak but we can do something about it. I can get some leaflets made up at college and we can hand them out to people over the next few weeks, tell them what's happening. Or we could get in touch with the press and shame these bandits publicly. There's loads of things we can do but let's not give up just like that."

"You don't know these people," Costello replied. "So I start another club somewhere else. It's no big deal, really. You can all come and work there when it's ready."

"Is that a promise?" Kathy shot back, "or are you going to let the Council decide who you employ or where you work? All of you lot," she said, turning to look at us all, "are pathetic. I really can't believe you're going to let them do this without a fight. Let's at least get a petition up."

"If you want to do that, then it's in your hands Kathy," Costello explained. "Meanwhile, we've got three weeks left before they move in. Now if you'll excuse me...."

Costello stood up and walked slowly to his office, closing the door gently behind him.

"Well," Jill said, "that's the end of that, then," and as everyone started to gather round, I picked up my newly acquired tunes and made for the exit sign, followed by Kathy who angrily stalked past me.

I figured she wasn't my biggest fan in the world as the Sandra debacle had won me few favours with the women in the club, but I at least wanted to applaud her spirit.

"You alright?" I asked.

"No, are you?"

She was grim faced and about to boil over.

"I just wanted you to know that I agreed with you back there. If you need help with anything you only have to ask."

"Is that why you kept your mouth shut in there?"

"I don't like to make snap judgements," I explained. "What are you studying, anyway?"

"The life and times of Fidel Castro," she told me and as she did something seemed to snap in her brain because she suddenly stopped walking and turned to face me.

"You might like to know that at one point Castro had an army of about twenty men fighting 30,000 soldiers. He didn't give in. He won the war. But then," she finished her history lesson by looking me up and down, "he was a man. See ya."

Kathy walked and, on an impulse, I decided to head up to nearby Regent's Park to find some peace and solace so as to gather up my thoughts whilst checking out the beautiful, and there is no other word, flower gardens they keep there which is one of my fave spots in town.

It was one of the boss things about this sprawling metropolis, for one minute you could be passing through an urban scenario so bleak that you wanted to shed a tear for all those families who had been crammed in and left to rot there, and then, before you knew it, you were standing in a nearby park, that was so serene and calming, it made you glad to be around to feel and see it all. I passed an hour away in the park with only my thoughts for company and what thoughts they were, a jumbled up kaleidoscope of mixed emotion and premonition for the future, and the realisation that just as my runnings had settled down to a very comfortable pace, life had once again upped the odds.

I couldn't help feeling that I was in static limbo, especially where work was concerned, for recently I had made up tapes of my some of my mixes and posted them off to a few pirate radio stations. That was weeks ago and I still hadn't heard a word, probably because the whole pirate scene was now overflowing with DJ's, all of whom had watched DJ groups, such as M/A/R/R/S or Bomb The Bass hit number one, and wanted in on the action. Costello's bombshell hadn't helped, either, for what if he didn't find new premises or, worse still, herded together a brand new staff to help him with his new venture.

Summer was starting to close in on me and I needed a voice to re-assure me, to tell me that every little thing would be alright, and their was only one canditate for the job. I went and belled Indigo.

"Hi, babe, what you doing?"

"Studying. You alright?"

"Not really, can I come over?"

"Why, what's up?"

"Just some news which I wish I hadn't heard."

"Well, give me a couple of hours to finish off this essay before coming. It should have been in yesterday. Is that alright?"

"Not really. I've got to go home and pick up my tunes. I'm working tonight."

"I'll pop down the club then. It's about time I did."

I didn't dare hesistate in my reply or Indigo, who is sharp when it comes to these matters, would have pounced on me straight away. She knew me that well.

"Well, it won't be a particularly great night. Wednesdays never are."

"That's alright, I feel like a bit of a night out. It feels like I haven't stopped working. I'll come for about ten, okay?"

"I might not be able to talk to you. JJ isn't coming down and I've got to do the whole shift."

"Scared I might not like your DJ'ing?"

"That isn't it."

"I'll check you about ten. You sure you're alright?."

"Yeah, I'll be fine. We'll talk later."

"You can tell me now."

"Nah, it's cool. But don't come if it's going to intefere with your study."

"I told you, I'll be finished soon. I wouldn't do that anyway. My degree is much more important than you are."

"Thanks, babe. I feel the same way about my record collection."

"Lonely wanker."

"Yes, indeed. Check you later."

"Bye darling."

As you know I didn't want to run the risk of Indigo coming to the club and hearing about the Sandra incident but now I had no choice for my hand had been forced, and so I promised myself that on this very night, after the dance was through, I would lay bare everything to her and damm the consequences.

That night, I reached The Unity early, set myself up in the booth and went in search of Jill who I found taking a quick drink at the bar before the faces started arriving in numbers.

"Jill, a friend of mine is coming down tonight..."

"Oh yeah," she pointlessly interjected.

"And I'd really appreciate it if no one mentioned Sandra or any of that business to her. Know what I'm saying?"

Jill arched her eyebrows. "Why not?" she asked.

"Because I haven't told her anything yet and I plan to lay it on her tonight, after the club. Can you help me out on this one?"

"I might be able to," she replied. "Sandra says you haven't been to visit yet."

"Yeah, well the best laid plans of mice and men and all that. I'm going to sort that out soon as well."

"Might be a good idea, loverboy."

"So not a word, okay?"

"I said, I'll see what can I do. Now, if you don't mind, both of us have got work to do."

I went back to the booth and started laying down some relaxed tunes, such as Lowrell's "Mellow Mellow," and Kool and the Gang's "Summer Madness," so as to build the calm before the storm, for DJ'ing is akin in some ways to the art of romping. You have to start off slowly, get everyone feelin' fine before you gear up with the tunes that you know will shake everyone into action.

I was just moving onto another level when Jasmine and Stinga appeared, both of them just popping in for an hour before heading off to Ronnie's to catch Art Blakey's last set of the night.

After the intros were through, Jasmine began skinning up whilst Stinga, still in his Thelonious Monk drag, stood quietly by. Just as Jasmine was lighting up the first of the night, Indigo appeared, dressed up in a very fetching outfit of Levi's cut offs and a white vest. I tried to keep down the nerves in my voice and made with the greetings.

"Hi baby. This is Jasmine and Stinga."

"Hi, pleasure to meet you. So this is where you get off to every week."

"Yep, this is the place and it's got three weeks of life left in it. Costello told us this afternoon. They're pulling it down."

"Is that true?" Jasmine put in.

"Afraid so."

It was at precisely that point that Jill made her entrance.

"Hello everyone," she announced in a voice that was far too cheery for its own good. "Heard about the club?"

"I was just telling them all about it."

"Shame isn't it? Still, life will go on."

I had no desire to introduce Indigo but it was one of those awkward moments when you have no option but to go against your better judgement, and so, "Oh, Jill this is Indigo. Indigo, Jill."

"Hi, I've heard a lot about you," she lied. "What do you think of his daughter, then. Beautiful isn't she?" You know those times in life when you have to tell yourself this really isn't happening to me, and you know that mix of growing despair when you realise that it is? Well, double that feeling and you now know exactly how I felt.

"I'm sorry," Indigo said, her face one of pure puzzlement. "Did you say daughter?"

"That's right," Jill replied as if nothing on this earth could be natural. "His daughter. Haven't you....Oh, I am sorry. That's me all over. Putting my foot in my mouth. Anyways, work to do. Good to meet you at last."

Indigo turned to me with an expression of such pure sadness and anger that it broke my heart in two just to catch sight of it, and that first night when she had cried in my arms after being betrayed flashed back to me.

I went to say something but Indigo stopped me right away.

"Don't," she commanded, before turning and walking straight out of the club. Jasmine passed me the spliff and then touched Stinga on the arm.

"I think we better be going. The set is starting soon. We'll check you later, alright? I mean, if you want to come round later, that'll be cool, you know."

"Thanks, I know."

"Take care. Come on, Stinga."

Mumbling his goodbye, Stinga and Jasmine departed, leaving me to it. I desperately wanted to go find Indigo but to be God's honest, I couldn't move a muscle for I was literally nailed to the floor and, for a few dazed and agonising minutes, I really didn't know what was what.

The club was now filling up and somehow I managed to get a grip and cue up the tunes but, boy-o-boy, was that the hardest night I've ever worked as I waited in a slow agony, constantly checking the watch, for the night to finish, all the time feeling as though my old world had just slipped away.

When the lights finally went up my first mission was to go in search of Jill and coat her off in a manner that she wouldn't forget for the rest of her life but, surprise surprise, the Bitch Brutus had exited early that night.

My next move was to make for the club's pay phone and bell Indigo but I already knew it was a fruitless exercise. Indigo would have snatched the phone off the hook and left it dangling the minute she reached her yard, a hunch of mine that was confirmed by the constant engaged tone I was forced to hear every time I punched out her number.

I thought of going round to see her but that gal would have died rather than let me in and, anyways, I didn't want to cause a scene for her, she already had enough on her plate.

Like the large comedown you experience after a night on the small white pill, I felt deflated, anxious and worried. It seemed that every time I went out into the world, fresh and hopeful, it maliciously conspired to send me back to my yard, beaten and bloody. It was then that I realised what a fool I had been to try and beat time. When you checked it calmly and objectively, it was obvious that Indigo would one day suss the kiddiwink scenario, and I had tried to stall the hour of her discovery. Time had beaten me soundly for my ignorance and I was now going to pay the cost.

That night, sleep did not come, blocked by the hot tears of regret that kept falling till the morning sun, and when they finally relented, a feeling of being so scared and alone bit so hard into me, that I even briefly contemplated ending it all then and there, but to take that step, an urge that I'm sure the majority of us all experience, takes a terrible amount of courage which only the few possess.

In the end, I wallowed in self pity, building a huge morning spliff and playing Bobby Womack's "Just my Imagination" over and over again, for the emotional push of the song caught my mood exactly.

The smoke seeped into my mind but if there is one thing about the spliff, or a lot of drugs, come to that, is that you can't fool with it if you're on a serious downer, for, like alcohol, it has a very nasty habit of amplifying everything that is bad in your runnings, building them up to ludicrous proportions in your mind's eye, and making everything seem a lot worse than it already is.

In this case, after the first smoke, my mind's solar system went askew, painting such a frightening future that I wished I could remove the smoke from my body and brain and start all over again.

I was conjuring up all kinds of bleak visions when the phone rang and I answered it quickly, desperate to hear Indigo's voice, hoping against hope that she would allow me a chance to clear up the mess that was now my life.

Instead I got Brother P.

"Yep."

"Some mutha fuckas have done over my sister. Come now. I'm over at Amanda's."

"Fuck, what happened?"

"Never mind that. Just get over."

"Don't do anything stupid, P."

"Just get over here. There's business to attend to."

"What number is she again?"

"34."

"I'm on my way."

Brother P. sounded charged up and defiant, and, not wanting him to make some rash moves, I quickly started to gather up my things, cursing the spliff that ensured I spent five minutes turning the flat upside down looking for my door keys when they were in my pocket all the time.

Finally, I was ready and, jumping on a bus to take me down the Stroud Green to the tube, and then eastwards to the Riversdown estate, I rushed over there in quick time.

I knew Amanda's pad from right back in the days when she had thrown a party to christen her new yard, and her family gathered together with friends, feasting on rice, peas and chicken, copious quantities of Appleton rum and Red Stripe, and a great selection of Jamaican tunes, ranging from ska to reggae, to see us through to dawn.

This was in the early days of the estate's life, when to get plotted up in Riversdown was a prestigious number, such was the hype surrounding its birth. The main attraction of these living quarters was a planned shopping complex which would ensure that everything you ever needed was ready and available just outside your door. The only problemo was that the complex was never build.

At the very last moment, the money boys suddenly pulled out, leaving the people who had move in stranded and forced to watch all their hopes and dreams collapse.

Firstly, the builders, as was only right, automatically downed tools once their wage packets were stopped, leaving behind the debris of their wasted efforts, a wasteland of rubbish from which these flats, only half of which had been filled, rose high above.

Then the real nightmare kicked in. The local council, desperate for accommodation, bought up the remaining flats and started to move in families that had spent years living in the scandal and squalor of bed and breakfast joints, run by unscrupulous landlords who raked in a fortune by charging exorbitant rent.

Many of the families lived four to a room, literally sleeping on top of each other, surrounded by the dirt and damp that attacked their health, living off a diet of cheap food and venting their frustration on one another in horrendous ways. By the time they had been relocated to Riversdown, it was too late.

Violence, alcoholism, hate and hopelessness was the normal fabric of their everyday lives. And that was just the parents for into the midst of this hell came the drug dealers, openly targeting the young, guessing correctly that here was a ripe area to exploit.

No one cares to admit that one of the prime reasons for taking drugs is pleasure, to enjoy the thrill of it all as they work their magic, and, for a few hours at least, make life a real high. That's a desire that crosses all class boundaries, from the beggar to the Crown, but when pleasure is in short supply, the need turns desperate.

Within a year of being abandoned, Riversdown started to suffer random outbreaks of violence as dealers and gangs started to fight for territory and control. Sporadic at first, the violence quickly escalated and then the unthinkable happened. The British National Party chose the site to open up a bookshop. Despite a wave of protest from some of the beleaguered residents, the unthinking greyers allowed the fascists their way, pointing out that we live in a democracy and therefore everyone has a right to express their views.

I get angered by such nonsense, really angered, for it strikes me that if you have something precious, which is what democracy, if practised to the max, undoubtedly is, you don't go and hand it over to the very people whose whole aim is to destroy it.

That's how you lose it and when the residents started receiving leaflets through their front doors, filled with hate towards anyone whose skin was not lily white and coursing with 100 per cent pure English blood – as if such a thing is possible – the battle lines started to appear.

Like the drug dealers, the BNP knew that here was a fruitful area of recruitment. Young impressionable kiddiwinks, bored out of their skulls, joined up because at that age it's anything for a laugh and some kicks to get you noticed, whilst some of their parents, eager to blame anyone but the true villain for their sorry plight, signed up as well, openly displaying BNP stickers in their dirt-smeared kitchen windows.

Amanda, and everyone else on the estate who understood that social living is the best, made constant pleas to the Council to relent on their democracy-for-all line and see sense, but the votes, like their fate, had already been cast. Even when an enterprising local journalist discovered that the council was secretly sending a car every morning to pick up a five-year-old name Sieta to take to school because her mother, following some threatening verbals from the local young ones, had withdrawn her from school, the story failed to sway the blind, indifferent council greyers.

Her mother, Mrs Punwabi, like a lot of the residents, lived in a state of complete twenty-four-hour fear, her every waking moment besieged by fright, the small sleep she was afforded besieged by apocalyptic visions.

She had been the victim of an arranged marriage, and, lacking the courage of a Jasmine at the time, had submitted to her parents' wishes. Her husband came from a village in North Pakistan, and he carried with him the dreams of his impoverished parents that he support them in their fading years by sending the valuable sum of £10 a week over to them. For them he was their only hope.

Unable to speak English, the husband had demanded that his wife be docile and obedient, following his every whim without complaint. In his religion, women should never work outside of the home, and so ingrained was this idea that he would countenance no other way.

Work was impossible to come by, and soon he was signing on.

Mrs Punwabi was forced to make good on the meagre money handed over, part of which was regularly sent to is parents.

One day she challenged him on this, pointing out that they could hardly feed themselves, let alone others.

His response was to break her nose. When she stumbled out of the flat to phone an ambulance, he dragged her back in and then beat her again. Then he forced himself upon her. Mrs Punwabi didn't speak for two weeks, and then, on the day he went to sign on, she summoned up all her courage, packed her bags and headed over to her parents' house to seek shelter.

At the front door her mother turned her away. She told her daughter to go back to her husband. She had caused a scandal on the family name and it would only be cleared if she went back to the man who rightfully owned her.

Luckily, a women's shelter was nearby and Mrs Punwabi desperately afraid, moved in. A month later, the morning sickness began. She was pregnant from her husband's rape. Word then reached her that he had been out and about searching for her.

When the Riversdown estate opened up, she was one of the lucky ones who was granted a home, and a few months later her child was born.

Yet, throughout this torment, Mrs Punwabi had found herself and started to change, questioning her ties to family, country and religion to cope with the everyday as best as possible.

When the BNP leaflets had started dropping on her mat, her response was to make up a series of posters that she plastered all over the estate, inviting the righteous to come to her flat for a meeting. Amanda, amongst others, decided to attend and on the very night that Indigo was walking out of my life, a group of them had crammed into her flat to discuss the crisis.

It was just as Mrs Punwabi had finished her first speech ever in front of a small crowd, and was sitting down as their warm applause washed over her that the bricks and stones came crashing through her second-floor kitchen window with a noise so frightful that everyone present literally jumped out of their skins.

"Where's the phone?" Amanda screamed as everyone ducked for cover. "There isn't one," Mrs Punwabi sobbed back, running to her child's bedroom where the sound of agonised crying could now be clearly heard .

Amanda and the rest of the group waited in a deathly silence to see what would happen next. But only a threatening quiet filled the room.

"I'm going to phone the cops," she announced.

"Don't," said a resident, a middle-aged guy who lived two floor up. "Wait a bit."

"They've gone," Amanda replied, listening out intently for signs of more activity. "My flat is only one floor up – I'll go get help."

Opening the front door slowly, Amanda slipped out, ran softly along the balcony, turned to go up the stairs, and smashed head-on into three guys standing on the stairs. Amanda screamed and swivelled as quick as she could to head back to Mr Punwabi's, but one of the guys caught her around the waist and they both fell back onto the floor.

"Keep her there, Jimmy," one of them shouted as he loomed menacingly over her, one of his hands reaching towards his flies. Amanda kicked her leg up as hard as she could and caught him square between the legs. He doubled up and fell against the stairs. The guy beneath Amanda let loose his grip momentarily and it was all she needed to struggle up, jump over the prostrate body of the guy she had kicked and bolt up the stairs.

As she did, she caught sight of the third guy who stood motionless throughout the whole incident, numb and scared.

"My God," Amanda remembered thinking to herself as she flew by, "he can't be any older than 10, if that."

She made it to her flat and desperately bolted herself in.

People, I have no idea where such virulent hate comes from. All I know is that violence begets violence. Kick a child from birth and he'll kick out for the rest of his life, so forgive the intrusion, but every time I picture Amanda in my mind's eye, struggling on that dirt cold balcony, or imagine little Sieta cowering in fright as the cavemen threaten her, anger clouds my vision and I can only see mankind as nothing more than an untameable, ferocious monster, intent on damaging themselves and everyone else. and it is then that all hope drains instantly away, and I am left temporarily without any belief in humanity.

From Clapham Common to Riverside, two worlds so far apart and light years away from each other, and all within spitting distance of each other, I could only pray that the Common Tribe would somehow prevail.

Amanda didn't call the cops that night. She spent the hours sitting against her front door, crying softly. At 6.30 she found herself able to move and called the one guy who would help – her brother. He reached her an hour later, and his sister insisted that he not call their father as his health had not been up to scratch of late and the worry could prove harmful.

That was when Brother P. belled me. But fate plays some very nasty blows when it has its wind up. Twenty minutes before I arrived, Amanda's father, Wilberforce, unexpectedly popped in on his way to work with some rum that his sister had just brought over to these shores, following her holiday in Kingston.

Unable to hide the consequence of the night before, for what parent cannot instantly pick up on a daughter's distress, the flat, when I entered, felt as if it was under siege. Wilberforce sat impassively in a chair, not saying a word, whilst his son paced the carpet, stopping every minute to peer out of the window to see if any of his sister's attackers were making themselves public.

Meanwhile, Amanda had retreated to her bed, worn out and

exhausted.

With his stocky guild and no-nonsense way, Wilberforce tended to dominate the space he was in, casting his mood – be that happy of sad – over the whole proceedings.

He had come from Jamaica to London in the early '50s, more out of loneliness than financial need, for, as a young man in his native land, he worked in a garage, quickly making his way through application and skill.

His work was outside of town and he would spend a week there with his boss before returning on a Saturday night to meet up with his family and friends. As his teenage years rolled by, he increasingly found himself attending farewell parties for an ever dwindling number of friends, lured to Britain by streets of gold promises from the government.

In the end, Wilberforce had no one to share a bottle of rum with, let alone go chasing the gals, so he too cashed in his chips and boarded the ship for England.

When he finally reached Waterloo Station, his old spa Dalston – so named because that was the area he was plotted up in – was waiting to greet him and show him the ropes whilst he put his runnings into gear.

He was soon shocked by the reception he got when he searched the paper for digs, and found averts stating that no coloureds, paddies or dogs need apply. Wilberforce had never before considered his skin colour a problem, but he soon sussed that the growing London Caribbean community was not to the liking of some of the natives, and had taken the place of the Irish as everyone's favourite whipping boy.

Undeterred, Wilberforce finally located a sympathetic landlady in Brixton whose only house rules were strict and regular payment of the rent and no Mighty Sparrow records blaring out at three in the morning, which was cool by him as he was a strict ska man and cared nothing for the sound of soca.

Dalston, meanwhile, had spotted a vacancy at a garage and informed his friend who duly went down there to enquire about employment.

The boss took him to a car and with a sneer asked him to diagnose the problem. Wilberforce examined the engine, spotted the fault and said so. The rattled boss would have none of it. He asked him for his qualifications. Wilberforce pulled out his Jamaican mechanic's certificate. The boss glanced briefly at it. "That's no good. It's not up to British standards. Sorry," and he walked off.

Two weeks later, Wilberforce was a bus conductor, working twelve hours a day and bitterly ruing his decision to leave Jamaica. London was not only strange and, in some quarters that he soon learned to avoid, hostile, but it was bitterly cold, the relentless wind biting through his very bones. To make matters worse, come winter time and the city would be continually covered in a smog so deep, created by the thick smoke that continually spewed out of chimneys, that sometimes you couldn't see your own hand in front of you.

Wilberforce dug in and after a year on the buses had just about saved up enough cashola to return home when he met Rose, his future wife, and, as love tends to do, altered his life irrevocably.

They met at a Joe Harriott gig at Ronnie Scott's one Friday night and fell for each other instantly. Within six months, Wilberforce had put his cashola down on a house in Hackney and they moved in, stretching themselves so much financially in these early days that sometimes there would be nothing but bread and water to nourish them.

It was here that Brother P. and Amanda were born and raised, their father exerting a strict check on them in their early years, instilling in them all those virtues and values that are such a drag as a bambino and which only start to make sense in later life.

As Wilberforce's motto was, do as I do and not as I say, he

enrolled in a night class and studied the ins and outs of the insurance racket. At first it was a hard slog. The subject was dense and puzzling, and he was nearly discharged one time when the guy sitting behind him started calling him a monkey every time his higher marks were announced, and Wilberforce nearly put a chair over his head, but, that aside, he passed his exams with good grades and quit the buses for good, starting up his own business for the benefit of his countryfolk, his original dream of returning home now fully restored in his mind.

He looked forward to the day he and Rose could return to Jamaica, breathe in the invigorating sea air and feel at one with the world once more. It was not that he hated England, because – no doubt about it – there was a tolerance amongst the majority that allowed him and his family to make their own way.

Wilberforce always acknowledged that because throughout his stay he had come across more decent than good and despite the terrible tragedies he had witnessed, the New Cross fire for example, he knew it was the work of the minority.

On that scale, things had greatly improved although it still remained a fact that there was only so far you could go before you were stopped point blank. The problemo was that you could never fit a face to the injury.

"Boy," I overheard him say one day to Brother P.,"in the old days it was different. People didn't like you, they'd tell you to your face. Nowadays it's different. You can smell it, you can touch it, but you will never see the person doing it to you. It's like a ghost that pops up once in a while to stop you in your tracks and then disappears before you can catch it."

Now we sat, silent and brooding, in his daughter's flat, because the enemy had come out of hiding and attacked with a ferocity beyond belief.

It was Wilberforce who finally broke the silence.

"Call the police," he told his son.

"What for?" came Brother P.'s reply.

"Never mind what for," he replied angrily. "I said call them."

Brother P., sighing loudly, went to the phone and belled the boys in blue.

"I want to report an assault," I heard him say. "It happened last night. Riversdown estate. You hear correct. My sister. Three guys. White guys. Yes, she did. No. How long will you be? As long as that? No, she can't come down to the police station. Number 34. Okay."

He put the phone down and with just a hint of sarcasm, added "They'll be here soon."

For three hours we waited around, the silence only broken by intermittent snatches of conversation. Finally there was a knock at the door, and Wilberforce went to answer whilst Brother P. roused his sister and brought her into the room, his arm thrown protectively around her.

Sitting down on the sofa, the two policemen, having turned down the offer of tea or coffee, sat opposite. The youngest of the pair pulled out his notebook, whilst his superior asked Amanda to relay her frightening fable.

After she had finished, the policeman asked, "Why didn't you call us last night?"

"Because she was too scared," interjected P.

"Let your sister answer if you don't mind," he replied, and Brother P. kissed his teeth loudly. His dad immediately glared at him and the younger copper adopted a glacial stare which he directed at P., who, on clocking it, responded with an equally icy look.

"Could you identify your assailants?" asked the interrogator.

"I think so, but things happened so fast..."

"And anyway," put in Brother P., not shifting his gaze from the fresh-faced boy in blue opposite him, "a lot of the racist thugs around here tend to look the same."

Wilberforce was on him in a flash. "Shut it, son. Let Amanda talk."

"Well," the copper replied, "let's not call them racist until we have all the facts in. It could well be that they were nothing to do with attacking..." – and he looked over to his partner's notebook – "Mrs Punwabi's house. It could be they were out mugging at the same time."

"That's the first time I've heard you guys call white people muggers," Brother P. said with a bite in his voice that had been been formed by his own unhappy experiences with the boys in blue. Too many times Brother P. had been pulled over in his car and interrogated as to how and why he was driving it, having to wait in frustration as they searched his vehicle from top to bottom before reluctantly letting him go.

"Son, leave the room," Wilberforce said with an authority that could not be denied. Brother P. looked at him and for one awful second I thought it would go off between them, there and then, and right in front of two coppers.

Praise the Lord it was not to be. Brother P. stood up and exited and I followed him out onto the balcony where he stood in a palpable rage for at least five minutes, looking down on the wasteland below.

"That's so typical of him," he finally said, "bowing down to those wankers in front of his own family." I knew better than to try and persuade him otherwise and so kept my counsel as we waited for the coppers to finish up and leave.

"Go back in there and make sure things are cool," Brother P. requested. "I'll be okay here." When I came back to the room it was to hear Amanda saying, "So you don't think it was racially motivated, Uh?"

"We didn't say that, Miss. As I said before, let's keep an open mind."

"So what are you going to do?" Wilberforce asked.

"Going on the description we have, we'll start making a few enquiries."

"You know, this is all your fault to begin with," Amanda said bitterly. "I wrote to both the council and your boss about that bookshop they've opened and I haven't had one single reply. There's a race relation law in this country but you lot just ignore it, don't you? Don't mean shit to your lot. I'm sorry, daddy, but it's true. You won't catch those scum. You won't even bother. In fact, I bet you're glad they're around – saves you the task, doesn't it? Now, if you don't mind, I've got a life to get on with."

"It's no good getting angry at us," said the older boy in blue, pulling on his cap. "It simply won't get you anywhere. Alright, love?"

Amanda simply stared them out as they packed up and left, Brother P. totally ignoring them as they pushed past him on the balcony. He watched their car slowly move away and then came back into the room where all three of us were gathered, lost in thought.

"I'll stay the night, sis," he announced to no one in particular. "No one else will protect you." He went into Amanda's bedroom and shut the door.

Amanda was the first to speak. "You didn't have to come over," she told me. "Thanks."

"No problem. I think it best I go now, yeah?"

Amanda softly nodded her head whilst Wilberforce sat firm in his chair as if he wasn't really with us and his mind had taken him to some place only he knew.

"Say goodbye to P. for me. I'll bell him tonight if that's alright."

"Sure."

I went to shake hands with her father, but Amanda signalled that such a gesture was meaningless, and so I exited, finding myself walking warily through the estate and its long passageways, keeping an eye out all the time for the local hoods but only clocking a variety of people of all ages and colour scurrying like small ants back to their homes.

It was now about four in the afternoon, but despite my tiredness I felt a strange surge of adrenaline pumping through me and on a strange high caused by tiredness and nervousness, determined straight away to go find Indigo and try and heal the wound.

I knew she would be at college today and so I made for Kentish Town and loitered with intent across the road from her building, calculating in my mind how I would best approach her and all the time adrenaline running riot in my stomach.

I hadn't waited too long when I saw her push through the revolving door, skip down the steps and make her way down the street. For a moment, I was tempted to let her pass and not do a thing, but before I knew it, I was running up behind her and tapping her on the shoulder.

She swung round and faced me, her normally happy face set in a stone cold expression.

"Indigo, we have to talk."

"No, we don't. There's nothing to talk about."

"Indigo, believe me, I was going to tell you that night," but as soon as my words came out, I kicked myself they sounded so feeble.

"Can we at least go for a coffee? All I want is five minutes with you."

"You had a lifetime to talk to me but you blew it. And right now I've got no interest in anything you have to say, now, tomorrow or in ten years' time."

"Don't say that."

"Tough. I just did."

"Look, at least give me a chance to explain."

"You don't have to. You're mistaking me for someone who

gives a shit. I really don't care."

"I do."

"Well, find another sucker to play your games with and tell them about it. You know, I must have been a bit crazy to think you were going to be different. But you're not. In fact, you're worse. Now, please excuse me. I haven't got time to stand around on street corners with the likes of you."

She turned on her heels and marched away. I ran after her, but just as I reached her, she suddenly twisted around and screamed, at the top of her voice, "Leave me alone!"

I stood dumbfounded as she walked slowly backwards, hate blazing in her large eyes where once I had only seen beauty and truth. Then she turned and ran.

I had not lost a lover but a true friend, and that in my book is the worst for sometimes this world can be so cold and deny you so much that in the end all you have to truly rely on is your close family of links and when one of them snaps, believe me, it will scar you forever.

Back at my yard, restless and at a complete loss as to how I could bring Indigo back into my world, I resisted the urge to call Brother P. and instead tried to bell her. The phone rang continuously, its relentless tone filling me with a quiet desperation. I tried her on the hour until, just as I was about to ring for the fifth time, my phone rang and I grabbed it quickly.

"How you doing, boss? I thought you were going to call."

"Shit, I'm sorry, P. How are things?"

"All quiet on the western front, I'm glad to report."

"I could come over if you need reinforcements."

"Not necessary. The natives are quiet tonight."

"How's Amanda?"

"Bearing up. We went up to see that Indian lady tonight. We're holding a march on Saturday. Can you make it?"

I had no hesitation in accepting my call-up papers, although it was immediately obvious that there was a very good chance indeed that our walkabout could end in bloodshed.

"We're having some leaflets made up. When you next playing at the Unity?"

"Saturday."

"Too late. I'll go down there tomorrow. Also, I'd be careful about bringing Indigo, if you know what I'm saying."

"Right."

My curt reply instantly gave the game away.

"What's up?" Brother P. asked and that's the trouble with people who know you well: you can run, but you can't hide. They catch you each and every time.

"I'll tell all when I see you."

"I'm in Westward Ho tomorrow. Meet me at Papa's about five?"

"No, don't worry about it. I'll see you Saturday."

"Not that. I want your help over this march, okay? So I'll check you then. Go well."

The next day, having seen off the night with only a couple of hours' sleep and feeling heavy from all the cigarettes I had been burning up, I made it over to Papa's where, much to my surprise, the Brother P. was already waiting, shooting the breeze with Marissa who was on her coffee break.

"Greetings all," I cheerily announced before ordering a capo and settling down, not failing to note the uneasy silence at the table.

"So how's the march preparations coming along?" I asked.

"Good. I'm picking the leaflets up in an hour."

"What match is this?" Marissa asked.

"It's a march to put right some wrongs," Brother P. replied, not caring to correct the gracious lady.

"You look pale," Marissa said, looking my face over with a kind concern. "You coming down with something?"

"No, I'm fine, really."

"He has a broken heart," cut in the Brother P.

"Yeah," I angrily responded, "how do you figure that one?"

"It's in the eyes," interjected Marissa, "it's always in the person's eyes. When you're happy they sparkle, when your sad it creeps all over your face. Paolo is the same and Papa."

"Help to talk?" Brother P. softly enquired and then I knew it was time to lay down my burden and fill both parties in with the sad and tragic details of recent events, and even though I understood that there was no easy solution, just the act of parlaring and laying it all out on the table did, in fact, help a little. I finished my unhappy fable and waited.

Marissa was the first to speak.

"Silly boy, eh? Silly boy. And the child? Do you see the child?"

"No, but I send money when I can."

Marissa gave me a little smack on the hand.

"Not good enough. Every child needs their parents. That's far more important than money. You have a child who needs you and you have to go to her. Never mind the mother, it's the child that's the only thing that is important here. Of course it's difficult, but that's the price for your fooling around.

"As for the girl who left you, why should she return when you hid all this from her? You're like a naughty child running away all the time. If you want my advice, then act like a man. Go see your child and be a father. If I was her that would be about the only thing that would impress me."

I sighed deeply. Marissa had told me what I somehow already knew, but had refused to act upon, and sometimes, when the truth is delivered and it hits you square in the eyes, once the sting has gone, you see your runnings in a light that was never there in the first place, and you wonder how you could be so blind.

It took me a day but that following night I belled Sandra..

"It's me."

"Yeah?"

She sounded sullen and tired and I began to see a fraction of the hurt that I had put upon her for it never once crossed my mind how it must be to raise a kiddiwink singlehandedly whilst having to keep your own life in the balance. All I had been worried about was my own runnings.

"How's it going?"

"What do you want?"

"Can I come over on Sunday?"

"And let us down again? I don't think so."

"I'll be there. I promise."

Sandra was silent and I could literally hear the suspicion taking over her mind.

"Look," I said slowly, "I know now that I haven't been up to much where you and Kimberley have been concerned. I'd just like to come over and spend some time with you both. I'll understand if you say no."

"I don't know," she warily replied. "I'll have to think about it."

"Well, call me as soon as you decide. If I'm not here, leave a message. Okay?"

"Alright, come over. But you let me down on this and I swear you'll never get another chance. You know I don't joke when it comes to my baby."

I swallowed the words 'our baby,' and instead said "I'll be there. I promise. Check you then, alright?"

"I suppose so. I got to go now. Kimberley needs washing and feeding. No doubt she'll get me up at four tomorrow screaming her head off so don't expect peace and chocolate when you get here, if you get here, alright?"

"Alright."

That night, I have to report, I slept better than I had done in days, the idea that I had finally started to get on top of events, no matter how small the progress, acting as a welcome sedative and seducing me into the darkness. It was then that I found my solar system unexpectedly whisking me back to teenage memories, the most specific being the day that my father made clear his intent to join a picket outside a local factory. He had decided on this action, God bless him, as it was heavily rumoured that a group of strike breakers, paid off by their bosses and protected by the boys in blue, were planning to drive their lorries through the line on this day. My mother had other ideas.

"You can't down go down there in your condition," she firmly stated. "You know what will happen. There will be bloodshed and violence and you'll end up in hospital."

"You're never too old to fight those bastards," he roared back but my mum knew better.

"If you go down to the picket line today then I'm off. I'm not going to wait around for you to come home in a coffin. Simple as that." They had no idea that I was standing in the kitchen catching their every word.

"You have to face facts. You're too old for this kind of thing."

"I'll be alright."

"You won't and you know it."

My father sat brooding in his chair all day, defeated by the passing of his years and his subsequent failing strength and, in my dream, I went to him and sat by his side in silence, holding onto his arm as if I could freeze him in time. I had been with him for what seemed like a minute when the alarm bell by my bed sprung into life and, in an instant, whisked me back to reality. I tried to close my eyes and re enter the dream but it was gone forever, and now it was 10. 30 a.m and time to rise up and head down to Riversdown.

As I dressed and prepared myself for the march, I tried to keep the thought of the day's threatened violence firmly at the back of my mind, for if I really considered the odds, then it was pretty certain that the cavemen would be out in force, blocking our every move.

To fire me up I put on "Fight The Power" four times as I got my shit together and, taking one last look around my yard, I headed out and onto the Stroud Green Road. The sun was well up by now and was strong enough to have allowed Digger, who sat on a pub doorstep, to strip down to just his grimy, cotton shirt, his overcoat laying across his lap, drops of beer dripping off the arm sleeve, as he pulled on a can of lager. As I passed, he raised his can in the air and gave me a salute and, I have to say, such a gesture considerably lightened my mood and, in an up frame of mind, I took the train to Riversdown.

As I had previously arranged, I met up with Brother P. outside the station and we made the short journey down to the estate.

"I think we'll get a good turn out today," Brother P. surmised, "we've had a good response. Now let's see if the words will be turned into action."

"Did you leaflet The Unity?"

"Yeah, I did an hour there and then I went to some other clubs, Legends, Astoria, and handed them out there. Most people thought I was handing out flyers for a club."

"Your reputation precedes you. Do you think there'll be trouble today?"

"Could be. I know the boys in blue will be turning out in full force. I brought you this."

He fished in his pocket and pulled out a small length of iron and then quickly passed it over before anyone could see.

"Is this neccessary?"

"Better safe than sorry. And, anyway, the harder they come..." Uneasily, I slipped the weapon into my inside jacket pocket and we made our way into the sprawling estate where the march was due to wind through, ending up outside the BNP bookshop in a mass protest. At the meeting point, a full crowd of about 700 had already gathered, containing a lot of familiar faces and numbers, such as the MP Bernie Grant who I always have a soft spot for, primarily due to his insistence on turning up at the opening day of Parliament, decked out in full African gears, the sight of which pisses off a lot of people, including most of his work mates.

To the left of him, I was surprised to check Daddy Cecil and his possee dressed up like the Black Panthers, sporting jeans, leather jackets, dark tops, berets and glasses, and there they stood in a rigid formation, impassively eye balling the assembled crowd of all shapes and sizes.

To their right stood members of the SWP, selling their weekly paper, rattling their cashola boxes in search of donations and filling the air with anti Government slogans. There was a palpable sense of excitement all around that you couldn't help get caught up in and as I was savouring the atmosphere, Brother P. called out, "Amanda, over here," and his sister made her way through the numbers.

"Hi everyone," she greeted us with and what a difference a few days make, for here she was looking alive and fresh, a sharp contrast to our last meet.

"Good turn out, eh?" she said to no one in particular, scanning the growing crowd. Unlike her brother, Amanda was tall for her age and thin with it, although sometimes, when she turned her head a certain way you would catch her brother's features.

"I spoke to mum this morning," she said, "she called just after you left the flat. She says dad is making plans to go back to JA for good."

"Really? He hasn't said anything to me."

"Would you go?"

Brother P. shook his head. "You're joking. This is my home."

"Same as that," Amanda replied.

"Has anyone seen the animals that attacked you?" I enquired.

"No, and nor have the police despite a name and three descriptions."

"Yeah, funny that," Brother P. put in. There was a shout from behind and we all turned to see none other than The Sherif and Jasmine, holding hands, and making a path to us.

"Alright?" they both breezily enquired.

"Good to see you both," said Brother P.

"So, come on then," Jasmine half shouted, "let's get moving and sort these wankers out. I want to get down The Unity tonight. It's your last night isn't it?"

"Yeah, until Costello finds another club. They're bringing in a load of special DJ's for the last night and for once in my life I want to enjoy myself there instead of having to work."

A voice, belonging to one of the women residents, and comically distorted by a loudspeaker, interrupted, informing us all to gather up as the march was about to commence.

By now, the numbers had swelled to about a thousand and banners, carrying slogans such as Black Under Attack and Stop The Fascists, shot up towards the sky as we started our journey, all of us knowing, deep down, that trouble was not far away. You could smell it in the air.

Two minutes into the march and it became reality. With the boys in blue marching alongside us, impassive to the shouts from the crowd that taunted them, we had walked along the estate's main thoroughway, hemmed in by the flats on either side.

It was just as the first marcher turned to go right that it happened; from out of nowhere the sky above went from blue to black and suddenly all manner of debris, picked like flowers, from the surrounding wasteland, was raining down upon us. The attack, I hate and have to admit, was brilliantly executed because not only did it send us into a whirlpool of panic, splitting up the bulk of the crowd, but it totally wrong footed the coppers, who now couldn't work out whether to leave their positions or not.

Some of the helmets made for the stairs to the building on the left, where, on the fifth floor, some twenty cavemen were hurling down their weapons of hate, and as they did, from behind us came a roar, and then there were 50 of them, piling into the crowd, scattering everyone to the side as they cut through the crowd, kicking out in all directions like Olympic sprinters gone crazy.

I quickly reached for my weapon just as a flying body stumbled into my back and sent us both to the floor. Luckily, I was the first to scramble up and without thinking, lashed out at the guy with my foot, just catching the side of his shaven tattooed head.

I moved off quickly while the women and their screaming kiddiwinks made for the relative safety of the flat entrances, to huddle up in inside. Tightening my grip on my weapon, the next thing I knew Daddy Cecil and his possee were rushing past me to attack the oncoming rush of caveman, smashing into them like surfers attacking monstrous waves.

I looked around for my friends but they had disappeared and now a surge of adrenalin was pumping hard into my heart, swarming into my bloodstream and taking away all fear. I moved as if I was on auto pilot, not even concerned for my safety, as I went to help Daddy Cecil and his crew. One of his men had been wrestled to the ground and was covering up his body as the caveman rained in kicks on his body.

I jumped the guy from behind and pulled him down, allowing the beaten guy to crawl to safety while I held him down. My opponent could not have been more than 16 years old but his face was creased up with such wild fury, that he become a human Rottweiler, a crazy fearless dog of war, and for a couple of seconds, I was totally transfixed by his terrible appearance. It was then that The Sherif intervened, pulling me away, and delivering a kick to the bollocks that had the young caveman squirming in agony.

"Come on," he said, "we're all over here."

I made to follow him but realised in a flash that I had dropped my weapon and, checking the ground around me, I had no chance to see the brick that came flying out of nowhere and which smashed into the back of my neck, sending vicious shots of pain up my head and knocking me into a pool of darkness.

When I came to, I don't know when, I was being carried by two boys in blue who gently laid me down inside the entrance to the flats. Outside, all I could hear was sirens merging with the loud and ugly noise of street violence and I felt sick. The adrenalin inside had turned to poison and what scared me further was that I could not raise my head.

"Right, what's wrong with you son?" I heard someone ask and, before I knew it, two St. John's Ambulance numbers were beside me, placing a thick pad of cotton wool under my neck and then lifting me onto a stretcher. They carried me into the lift and then along a balcony before turning into a flat that was now acting as a makeshift hospital.

"Put him down there," I heard a voice say. I looked up to see a thin faced Indian women approaching me.

"It's just slight concussion," one of the ambulance numbers said, "and we've stopped the bleeding. Just keep him still and he should be alright." There in the room, a young man sat on the sofa holding a wad of tissues to his nose, his head bowed in pain. On the chair opposite sat little Sieta, looking at us both, one to the other, with a frightened wonderment. Her mother came into the room with a new swab of cotton wool that had been dripped in something.

She came to me, lifted my head up slowly, moved away my original bandage, and placed the swab on my wound, causing a fiery sensation to spring up in my neck which quickly and mercifully disappeared.

"How many fingers can you see?" she unexpectedly asked, placing three, elegant long fingers in front of me, and it brought a smile to my face because it's the kind of thing you see in those dumb cop shows on TV, and you never think for one minute that one day you'll be going through the routine.

"Three," I replied.

"Where are you?"

"In your flat." Mrs. Punwabi smiled. "I think you'll be okay."

"I still feel a little sick."

"I'll get you a pillow and you can rest up." Once I was slightly propped up I could take in more of the small living room where photographs of Sieta adorned the walls and surfaces, documenting the child from birth to now, providing a personal history of time and beauty. Outside, the noise had thankfully started to die down and reasoning that at any second there might be more urgent casualties than myself, I pulled myself up feeling a lot of better than I figured I would. The guy on the sofa still had his head bowed down low.

"You alright, mate?" I asked him.

He didn't look up but said, in a low voice, "I wish I had never got involved."

It was then that he looked up at me and my heart went into a minor shock. 14 years old, if that, with his hair cropped close, he was, unbelievably, one of the enemy and here was Mrs Punwabi attending to his wounds.

"I wish I had never got involved," he repeated and then he bowed his head again and gave out a little sob. I moved into the kitchen where Mrs. Punwabi, and two other women, who I didn't recognise, were standing.

"You shouldn't be up," Mrs. Punwabi remonstrated.

"I'm okay. Really I am. That guy you've got in there..."

"We know," said one of the women, "but he's just a baby. There's no problem."

"Thanks for all you've done," I said to Mrs. Punwabi. Indeed, I wanted to tell her that this country and town was so much better off with the likes of her around but such speeches are best left unspoken, so I gave her a small hug, bade her friends goodbye and wandered out onto the balcony to survey the scene below. It was obvious that the boys in blue had now seized control of the situation. Large pockets of them roamed up and down the mainway, a blue caterpillar scouring the ground for suspects.

I ventured upstairs to Amanda's flat hoping to catch up with my links, praying that they had not been damaged, but as there was no answer there, I caught the lift down to the ground floor and made my exit out of the back door, not wanting to meet up with any boys in blue.

As I made my way to the train station, furiously debating as to the location of my friends, I decided a cab would be the best way of transport, and, as I had previously noticed a mini cab office nearby, I set sail for there, reaching within two minutes. I walked into the small, shabby office and there, sitting anxiously on a small wooden bench was a gal who I vaguely recognised. I looked at her for just a little too long and so had to say something as she was now looking at me with great inquistiveness.

"I know you don't I?" I asked her. "Were you just on the march?"

"Yes, I was. Now I'm trying to get to the hospital but they say they haven't got any cars."

As if on cue, a driver unexpectedly walked in and bade her come with him. "Look," I said, having not thought at all about this option, "can I come with you? I've lost my friends and they may be up there."

"Sure." She motioned to the swab I was still holding to my head.

"You look like you need treatment yourself."

"It's nothing. Looks worse than what it is."

"Let's go then."

On the way there, I asked after her boyfriend.

"Do you know if he's badly injured?"

She shook her head.

"I wasn't meant to come here today, he asked me not to as he said there would be trouble. But I had to. I woke up this morning with a horrible feeling that something would go wrong, and now it has. I hope to God he's okay. I saw him being taken into an ambulance just as I got to the estate and so I dashed up here."

"I'm sure he'll be fine. A lot of the time injuries look a lot worse than they actually are," I lied.

"What do you do, by the way?"

"I'm a journalist," and when she said it, everything just clicked into place. No doubt about it, this was the gal that had turned up to interview Daddy Cecil in the Portobello cafe all those months ago. Just to make sure I asked,

"What kind of things you scribble on?"

"Lifestyle stuff basically but my main thing is a book on the history of West Indian politics in Britain. My boyfriend is helping me out with it."

I kept my silence but inside I couldn't help but smile. It would be the perfect ammo next time the Daddy man started in on me.

"What about yourself?" she said but so anxiously was she scanning the road ahead, impatient to reach her loved one, that I knew she was just making small talk.

"Oh," I replied, "I wish to become a missionary and realise Heaven's promise. That's all."

"Sounds nice," she said, still staring ahead.

A minute later we were in front of the hospital desk, where a nurse informed us that a Cecil Smith had been admitted but it was nothing too serious, and as for the names I had handed over, only one was present and correct. I found The Sherif and Jasmine sitting in the casualty waiting room. He wore a bandage around his head and Jasmine clasped his hand tightly. They made for the perfect couple.

"Hey," shouted The Sherif as I came in, "another accident of war."

"How you doing?"

"He's doing fine," Jasmine said, "aren't you, petal? We're going to get you nicely bandaged up and then you'll be fit for action, once more, if you know what I'm saying."

She laughed loud, so did The Sherif and so did I. It felt like the first time in ages that I had cracked open a smile.

"You going to be alright for tonight?" The Sherif asked me. "You don't want blood dripping all over your tunes."

"I'll be cool. And you?"

The Sherif winked at me.

"Raring to go, my friend, raring to go. Nothing like a decent afternoon's rumble with scumbags to set you up for the night."

"Where's P. or Amanda? I haven't checked them yet."

"The cops pulled Amanda and P. went down there to bail her out. He told me to tell you that he'll check you down the club."

"Are they alright?"

"I should say so. P. clobbered quite a few of them before they got Amanda. Ten nil to us, I reckon."

"Ten-two," Jasmine said, looking at the both of us.

"I better split. You'll be okay?"

"Nothing we can't handle."

I belled a cab from the hospital pay phone and as I was waiting for the car, I thought of popping in briefly on Daddy Cecil and embarrassing the hell out of him, but as he and his boys had been right in the thick of it all, I resisted.

He and I would always go our separate ways, that was for sure, but we'd joined up when it mattered and you can't say better than that. The cab arrived and, checking the time, I decided, on a whim, to go visit Papa's as a great hunger had now taken the place of the sickness and needed dealing with, fast. Papa was just starting to close when I reached but one sight of the swab I held to my head and he was calling out to Marissa to fetch the first aid box, making me sit still as a statue as he personally attended to the dried up wound placing a huge plaster over its ugly face.

Just as he had finished there was a tap at the window and there stood Brother P. and Amanda, smiling away, motioning Papa to open the door. For the next hour, as Papa and Marissa organised food, we sat around the table, relating the day's events, with the Brother P. confirming that five of the caveman would be waking up tomorrow with eyes the colour of his skin.

"Couldn't do much more because this one started in on that copper we met. You know the young bolshy one? Amanda told him to his face what she thought of him and his parentage."
"Yeah, he deserved it," she chimed in proudly. "So it was all down to the cop shop to bail her out."

"And?"

"No charges, believe it or not," she informed us.

"I've got to tell you about Daddy Cecil, P. but you must keep it quiet for the time being."

After I relayed the fable, Brother P. leant back in his chair.

"You see," he said, "John Thomas does have his uses after all. He may well be the best bet ever for race relations in this country."

Papa entered from the kitchen expertly carrying plates of steaming spaghetti bolognese on both arms, which he placed in front of us, and we dug in like this was the last supper, polishing off everything laid before us in complete silence, except for that delicious sound of food being enjoyed by each and every one.

It was just as the cappuccinos arrived that Paolo turned up, walking in with his ever present football bag slung over his shoulder.

"I'll get your dinner," Marissa said, departing for the kitchen and leaving the only vacant seat, right next to Papa. The young man sat down and Papa reached over and poured him a glass of wine.

"You have a game tomorrow?" he enquired of his son.

"Yes, Papa," Paolo warily replied, taking a sip of wine and not even looking his father in the face.

"What time?"

"Two 'o' clock kick off."

"Good. I'll take you there after mass." Paolo went to say something, I know not what, but Papa raised his hand and silenced him.

"Your friends have been in the wars today," he said motioning to us. "Perhaps they will tell you all about it."

Fortified by the food and the company, it was such good fortuna to sit around the table, safe and satisfied as we all put in our pennyworths and filled in Paolo on the incredible roller coaster of events, his eyes growing even larger when some of the incidents were described. I could have sat there all night but a check on the watch told me that it was time to head homeways, pick up my tunes and make it to The Unity for my last session there. As Brother P.s four wheeler was parked outside, we made with the kisses and the ciao's ciao's to the Supinos, for they had treated us like their own, and clambered in and made our way back to my yard.

As I was getting my tunes together, and feeling like I had been up for two days already, Amanda turned on the TV and when the news came on, they flashed up a brief report on Riversdown. It was strange to see the battle from various TV angles and as we looked for each other in the melee of crowd shots and running coppers, I suddenly started thinking, for no apparent reason, of all those numbers, living out in England's quiet country villages, who right now would be clocking the screen in outrage and wondering out aloud to their families about whatever happened to the good old days. No doubt, they would cluster, that very night, down at the local Tory bar and shout at the top of their voices for national service and flogging to be brought back in, not realising that the good old day, if it ever really existed, was gone and buried, and that, in fact, it was far more dangerous to walk their streets alone than ever it is mine.

Forgive these ponderings for now it was time to split and, ignoring the twenty or so messages on my answer machine requesting that their names be put on the guest list, we lugged my record boxes down the stairs, and made for The Unity. When we reached, a large crush of faces and numbers, bright and youthful, crowded around the door.

Luckily, Rajan spotted us and we squeezed through the space he created and into the club where J.J. had already started spinning. I dumped my tunes by him and went for a little walkabout. The first cat I bumped into was Stinga, sporting a distinct Malcolm X. look and standing solo. I still didn't know what had gone off between him and Jasmine and so had no inkling to tell him that I was with her and The Sherif some hours ago.

He couldn't tell me either as the Malcolm he had chosen to copy was the fiery, white hating Malcolm, the one yet to make the trip to Mecca and change his ways, and so, he half-apologised, for the next month or so, he could not be seen rapping with me. "Fair enough Stinga," I answered back and then moved off having spotted Davey Boy, drinking on his own at the bar.

"Davey, how goes your percentage of life?"

"Up and down, soldier, up and down."

"Lord Haw Haw not with you tonight?"

"He's inside."

"Prison?"

"Yeah, smuggling E's the stupid bastard." Davey Boy took a huge gulp of his drink, wiped his mouth and said, "You would have thought that someone has caked up as him wouldn't have to do that shit, wouldn't you?"

"I know but pater and mater will bail him out surely."

"Oh, his uncle will probably be the judge sentencing him."

"And the group?"

"Going strong. If I can get them off the happy pills for five minutes, we might even get a record out one of these days. I don't know, it's just stress all the time these days," and for the first time ever, I saw something of the real Davey Boy come to light, but it was gone in a flash and the cheeky Cockney mask went back on.

"Still, I haven't forgotten your tonik number," he happily said. "I'm going to see someone next week, reckons they've got a warehouse full of the stuff."

"Yeah, alright Davey. I'll pop in at the end of the week, okay?"

"You do that son," he replied, "you do that."

It was time to man the dex one last time although, in the excitement of the past days I had been unable to put any thought towards this last set, and in a way I was glad I hadn't for sometimes when you plan something too well, it has a tendency to backfire on you. I just opened up my box and pulled out tunes at random, throwing it all in, mixing up rare groove with house, rap with soul, jazz with reggae, and not caring that the tunes followed no party line. The crowd, I'm happy to report, were of the same persuasion, parting only once to allow Sammy The Foot and his crew space to dazzle everyone, a spectacle that I was glad to see his gal, watching from the sidelines, enjoying immensely.

I finished up with a tune that I am convinced was written when God was in the room because how else can you explain the spirtual power and musical grandeur of The Staple Singers' "If You're Ready (Come Go With Me)."

My fave bit is towards the record's end when the music goes up a notch and Mavis Staples starts testifying about a land where there is "no economical exploitation, no political domination," a place we should all be fighting to live in. When the record ended and the lights came up, Brother P. came up to the booth with Amanda, and put his arm around me.

"I've made a few moves tonight," he said in his quiet manner. "If we play the cards right, we'll be sorted. We'll speak tomorrow?"

"Of course we will," I replied, giving him a little hug, glad that I had kept such an ally by my side throughout the years, knowing that there were still so many more mountains for us to climb.

"I'll check you then. Seen?"

Amanda gave me a kiss on the cheek.

"He won't say it but you were slammin' on the dex tonight," was her passing comment. I collected up my tunes and then made straight for the cloakroom where I expected to see Jill who I still wanted to parlare badly with.

"She quit," Rajan said as I clocked a brand new face behind the counter, handing out the last of the coats. "Flew the nest last night," and all things considered that was probably the best thing for both of us.

"Did Jasmine make it down?" I enquired of her brother.

"There were so many people, I didn't get to see everyone."

"Nah, I didn't see her or the psycho all night."

"Where's Costello?"

"In his office." I went over and pushed the door to. Costello sat at his desk, a huge wad of cashola piled up in front of him.

"Ah, come in, young man, come in. I have a treat for you."

He handed over double my usual wages.

"For services rendered. Keep in touch, I want you for my new club."

"Thanks a lot, boss," I replied, "I'll certainly do that."

"And don't bring any babies again, promise?"

"I promise."

"Ok, off you go."

There was a party going on back at someone's yard that I had been told about but I had a major mission to attend, so grabbing a mini cab from outside, I went back to my yard, kept the car waiting, rushed upstairs, dropped off my tunes and as a beautiful, purple dawn started to break across the sky, I directed the driver to a north address.

It is always funny driving down an empty street that you know in a couple of hours will once again awake to city street drama, a stretch of buildings and concrete that will no doubt be standing after each and every one of us has long since departed this earth, headed hopefully for a better land. Mother and baby were fast asleep when I reached their front door and it took five minutes of gentle knocking and whispering loudly through the letterbox to rouse Sandra.

"What are you doing here so early?" she demanded in a sleepy voice, clutching her gown around her.

"I'm sorry, I couldn't sleep and I wanted to see Kimberley."

"I said, this afternoon."

"I know Sandra but now that I'm here...."

"Alright." She let me in and closed the door, and I followed her into her room. "Don't make a sound," Sandra whispered. "I've only just got her back to sleep. You wake her and there'll be hell to pay." Sandra climbed back into her bed and I stepped over to gaze on my daughter's sleeping face, so unworried, so contented and so unbelievably beautiful. I swallowed hard and I felt the tears building up behind my eyes and no matter how much I fought them, it was no use and they began to streak down my face until in the end I had to turn away to go wash myself in the bathroom.

As I washed the tears away and patted my face, Kimberley came to life for I suddenly heard her cry, like an ambulance siren as it goes off for the first time, and when I returned, Sandra was sitting up in bed, breast feeding her. I acted cool but truth be told the scene flustered me, so I went out to the kitchen to prepare some coffee. A minute later Sandra walked in.

"Here," she said, gently placing our daughter in my arms, "she needs changing and I've run out of nappies. I'm going down the shop. Don't panic," she said, noting my expression, "she won't bite."

I took Kimberley into my arms and rocked her, not even daring to talk whilst Sandra dressed and then left for her provisions. The minute Sandra left, an impulse, from out of the nowhere blue came into my mind's solar system, and I quickly made for the phone and with one hand, I dialled a familiar number. Four rings later, a sleepy female voice came onto the line.

"Hello...who's this?"

"Indigo, I'm standing here holding my daughter. I just thought you should know."

Then I put the phone down and kissed my daughter's head.